THE PRYCE OF DELUSION

An Historical Ghost Cozy Mystery

THE PRYCE OF MURDER PREQUEL

KARI BOVÉE

CHAPTER 1

JUNE 3, 1879
PRYCE THEATER, NEW YORK CITY, NY

Satiated and with a hum of euphoria coursing through me at delivering another satisfying performance, I twirled the ring on my right hand ring finger. It was a gift from my father. A talisman of sorts. The gold, heart-shaped ring, with a lovely Forget-Me-Not flower fashioned from diamonds in the center, never let me down and I was never without it on stage.

Usually, after the final curtain call, I retired to my dressing room where I removed the ring and replaced it in a jewelry box that I kept in a drawer in my vanity. I felt it would bring bad luck to wear it anywhere but the stage. But, tonight, after the dozen curtain calls my audience demanded, my fellow thespians swept me directly into the greenroom to celebrate our successful show debut.

Maurice Merriweather, my leading man, had just uncorked several bottles of champagne. He played the wily Robin Hood to my Maid Marian in the little-known play, *Sherwood Forrest,* an adaptation of an obscure French play written in the seventeenth century.

He was pouring a round for some of the cast and crew with the help of Mr. Potter, the theater's Rigger, who was responsible for the booms, lifts, hoists and backdrop rigging.

"My fair lady, Arabella!" Maurice approached me with two champagne glasses in his hand, one of which I assumed was for me. "It is always a pleasure to be on the stage with you."

Maurice was a dashing young man with smoldering dark eyes, a strong jaw, a most charming cleft in his chin, and was half a decade my junior at twenty-five. However, his love of drink, and his reputation as ne'er-do-well sot, made him seem and look much older. It had also done much to prevent him from getting roles. He had been out of work for several months.

Aside from the fact he was often late for rehearsal, and would occasionally show up drunk with a scandalous woman on his arm, he was brilliant and his audiences adored him. On a wing and a prayer I had encouraged the director to cast him, and judging by the success of tonight's opening performance, I did not regret my actions.

However, we were planning to go on tour in four months, after the run here at my theater, and I would not be taking Maurice. He was too much of a liability to take on the road. At least here I had some control over him. He did not know this yet, of course. Mr. Blackstone, my theater manager, had given the rest of the company their contracts and they had all been signed. I would have to break the news to him soon, before he found out about the others, but I wanted to get into a rhythm with the show first.

I reached for one of the champagne glasses in his hands, but instead of giving it to me, he took a sip from it, and then did the same with the other. Apparently, they were both for him.

"Same," I said, deciding to ignore his rudeness.

"You were both wonderful, darling." William, my husband, who had so generously purchased the theater for me and had given it our name, The Pryce Theater, strode up to us. "The chemistry between you is infectious!"

"William!" I said, astonished. "What are you doing here? I thought you were headed to Colorado tonight."

"My trip has been delayed. One of the freight trains on the route careened off the tracks. Apparently, it's a terrible mess." "I'm rescheduled to go out on Thursday."

William today looked every bit the consummate, wealthy business man, with his finely made suit and patent leather lace-up shoes. When I'd first met him, I had been drawn by his air of confidence, and his classic good looks. He had a strong brow and chin, a thick but well-trimmed mustache, and dark blond hair peppered with gray.

His latest business venture, and one that I daresay had become quite an obsession, was a hotel he had built in the small, backwoods, and primitively uncultured Colorado mining town called La Plata Springs. I had never been there, and from what I'd heard thus far, had absolutely no intention of ever going. He'd asked me to accompany him on several occasions, but I had no desire to travel to the untamed West where all nature of wild animals roamed, and battles were continually fought between the native peoples and those who wished to conquer them. For the life of me, I did not understand the appeal.

Maurice raised both of his glasses and then gave a theatrical bow, sweeping his Robin Hood hat off of his head.

He loved that hat and had come to wear it at all times when in the theater. I supposed it made him feel close to the character. He'd even adorned it quite differently than the real Robin Hood might have. Instead of a pheasant feather in the band, he'd replaced it with two small ostrich feathers. Quite extravagant, and not at all appropriate for Robin Hood, but that was Maurice.

"Thank you, kind sir," he said. "Your wife makes all of us look good out there."

Cordelia, my assistant and dear friend had accompanied William and she came to stand at my side. Silently, she hooked her arm through mine and gave it a little squeeze. Her fresh and befreckled face beamed with happiness for me.

"Yes, thank you, dear," I said to my husband.

We had been married for five years. It was not a love match, but one of mutual respect, friendship, and convenience. He supported me in whatever I chose to do, thus the theater, and spared no expense for my comfort and lavish lifestyle.

"I anxiously await my contract for the tour," Maurice dropped in randomly, giving me a pointed stare. My stomach turned. So, he'd heard that the contracts had been issued.

William cleared his throat, clearly uncomfortable at this declaration. He, Mr. Blackthorn and I had made the decision together that Maurice's understudy, Theodore Brinks, would join me on tour instead. I looked over at William imploringly. He gave me a barely imperceptible nod and took Maurice by the elbow.

"May I have a word . . ." He led him away.

I worried that once Maurice knew the truth about the tour, he would walk away from the show, thus disappointing his local fans, but Mr. Blackthorn said it was of no concern. The man could not find work, and he needed this role.

"Mrs. Pryce?" Rebecca Poitier, a young black woman who was my stage dresser and costume mistress, gently tapped me on the shoulder. "May I speak with you?" She was carrying my new little Havanese puppy, Bijou, in her arms. I reached for the pup and she nearly jumped into my embrace. She enthusiastically licked my chin. She was a darling little puff ball and I was completely in love with her.

With a tilt of her turbaned head, Rebecca beckoned me to retire with her to a quiet corner.

"Is everything all right?" I asked.

Her diminutive countenance, with large dark eyes and mocha skin, had taken on a disturbing expression.

"Yes, ma'am. But, he's back. You know, the man who has

shown up at a few of your stage rehearsals? He was waiting for you outside your dressing room door."

"Oh dear, yes. What does he want?"

She was referring to a rather enthusiastic fan of mine. He'd been seen in the back row for a few of our rehearsals with a bouquet of roses in his hands. Mr. Blackthorn, used to dealing with my followers, had quietly escorted him from the theater. We agreed he seemed perfectly harmless, just a little besotted, which I must admit was flattering.

"To see you," she continued. "I told him you were indisposed —that you were busy, but he was insistent. He's now standing outside the green room door."

I rolled my eyes. "Oh dear. Very well. I will speak with him." I complied. "Please do join us for the party, Rebecca."

She gave me a warm smile. "Thank you, Mrs. Pryce. But, I really must get on. Althea is still not well, and it is a lot to ask of Priscilla to take care of her."

"Oh dear, I do hope she gets better soon."

Recently widowed, Rebecca had three girls, one of whom was sickly. Her eldest daughter, a child of twelve, was often left home to care for her two sisters while Rebecca worked to make ends meet.

Together we walked to the greenroom door. When we reached it, I handed little Bijou back to Rebecca.

"Would you take her to her bed in my dressing room? I'm afraid the party in here might be too much for her."

"Of course." She gathered the puppy in her arms again.

We found the gentleman patiently sitting in a chair that had been placed against the wall. He sprang to his feet, and came over to me in a rush. He was a handsome man, with a head of loose dark curls, and a boyish grin.

"Mrs. Pryce! Another astounding performance!" He thrust a bouquet of red roses toward me.

"Thank you, Mr. —Forgive me, I've forgotten your name."

"Hughley, Daniel Hughley," he said with a glint of keenness in his eyes.

I offered my hand. He took it and planted a faint kiss upon my knuckles. I noticed that he kept his other hand tucked in the pocket of his coat. It was a well-made coat, if not last season's designs, but nice nonetheless. He had an odd-looking boutonniere on his lapel made from some kind of fluff. The scent of the roses mingled with another, also pleasing, emanating from him. It was a mixture of fruit and dry spice, like cloves—or perhaps cinnamon. He pulled his face away, but did not let go of my hand.

"What a lovely ring," he said, admiring it. "Is this the one you always wear on stage?"

I blinked at him in surprise. "Um. Yes—how did you?—"

"I read the story about you in *The New York City Times*. I didn't realize you were the daughter of the poet, Alastair Janes."

"Oh," I said, remembering I had mentioned it in the interview. "Most people don't." I slipped the ring off my finger and handed it to Rebecca. "Please put this away, would you, darling?"

Rebecca gave me a brief nod. "Yes ma'am. Goodnight." She left and I was alone with Mr. Hughley.

"Mrs. Pryce—may I call you Arabella?"

I blinked again at his boldness.

"Arabella," he proceeded in a rush. "I can no longer go on without professing my passionate admiration of you. I confess, I think about you often. I feel we have a strong connection—and when you are on stage, it is as if you are speaking to me and to me alone."

I sucked in a breath, about to retort at his impertinence, but he held up a finger to silence me.

"May I request the privilege of having you accompany me to dinner some time?"

Stunned, I struggled with a response. Finally, I found my bearings.

"Mr. Hughley, I am a married woman."

He gave a little shrug. "That doesn't mean that we can't—"

"And faithful to my husband," I added.

He frowned. "I see. Forgive me."

It was not unusual for me to receive the odd love letter, or flowers and gifts from gentleman fans, but this was quite bold.

Someone came up from behind him. It was my mother.

"Arabella?" she queried. From the tone of her voice I could tell she knew something was amiss. "Who is your friend?" she asked cautiously.

"He is not my friend. Merely a fan." I answered. I looked the man straight in the eye and handed back the flowers. "Good evening, Mr. Hughley."

The muscles of his jaw twitched and the set of his full lips hardened to a thin line.

My mother fixed him with a glare. One I had received many times, and it provoked a most unpleasant feeling. Mr. Hughley raised his chin, dropped the bouquet to the floor, turned on his heel and left.

CHAPTER 2

"What was that about, Bella?" My mother asked, using the moniker that made me flinch. She often used it when she wanted something, or rather, wanted to manipulate me into something.

"It was nothing," I answered. "Just a fan who had overstepped his bounds. Shall we join the party?" I asked, not wanting to engage in a private conversation—as I knew what it would be about.

William and I had discussed his replacing her as my manager, and I knew my mother sensed the change coming. Her behavior toward me had become even more disdainful, and I dreaded her finding out the reality of it. In some way, I would pay for my transgression. No one crossed Millicent Janes without repercussion.

"You look distressed, darling. Shall we retire to your dressing room? I'd like to speak with you about the performance."

I gritted my teeth. "Must we right now? I'd like to go to the party."

"Something needs to be done about Maurice. He overacts. I wish you had taken my advice and had hired Paul Davidson."

I sucked in a breath, trying to hold my temper, not wanting

to give in to this conversation, but finding myself drawn in, which was even more vexing. "Paul Davidson is otherwise engaged. I told you, Mother."

"But, surely, you could have changed his mind. Money talks, after all."

"For all of his faults, Maurice has a huge following in New York." I countered.

"Come now, Arabella—"

I straightened my spine. "Mother, enough."

Her mouth fell open at my admonishment. It was something I never did, but the condescension of her tone, another trait I was all too familiar with, threatened to push me over the edge. She had always been overbearing when it came to my performances and my career, but for this particular show she had been at her most irritating best.

"I beg your pardon?" She narrowed her eyes at me.

"You have had something to say or questioned almost everything about this play, from the choice of play, to the choosing of the cast—which the director was none too happy about I might add, all the way down to the costumes and lighting. For goodness sake, you even went up onto the catwalk to inspect the positioning of the backdrops, which really is none of your concern and quite dangerous!"

Her mouth still agape, snapped shut. "I only want what's best for you and your reputation, Bella."

"I, and my reputation are fine, Mother."

"Well, not if you let that stage ham run riot," she said under her breath.

"Mother," I said, a little more calmly. "I don't wish to quarrel with you. Can't we enjoy the evening? The audience loved the show. They loved Maurice. There is nothing more to be said."

"He's not accountable, Arabella. And, the crowd he runs with —you don't want association with him."

"Please," I said. She was right, of course, about his not being accountable at least, and William and I had that in hand, but I didn't want to discuss it with her now. Or ever.

She set her mouth in a thin line, but didn't say anything more. However, I had a feeling she would not be silent for long. She never was.

I put this more ardent-than-normal dogmatism down to her intuition that things were about to change with William, and me, taking more of an active role in my career, and she was grasping at any last bit of control she might have.

"I'll fetch you some tea, and we can continue this in your dressing room," she persisted.

I bit my lip to prevent myself from lashing out at her.

"No, but thank you. I'd like to join the others."

She graced me with the same glare she had just offered Mr. Hughley. "Fine. I'll wait for you, there. Take your time."

I sighed with irritation and rejoined the party.

At first, my mother had been smitten with William—or rather his wealth—and had done everything in her power to see us married.

After my father left us to pursue his poetry and bohemian lifestyle in France, my mother made it her mission to escape our poverty and set me upon the London stage, at age ten, to make a living for us. Luckily, I had talent and became much sought after by directors and producers. By the time I was twenty, I had become wildly famous in Europe.

I credited some of my success to the lovely ring my father had given me. He told me it would bring me luck if I wore it on stage, and it had. I would occasionally receive a letter from him, but had not seen him in years. He was the one with whom I shared a kindred spirit. My mother and I, on the other hand, were like oil and water.

Once we were somewhat financially secure, my mother's plans to see us improve our station even further with an association with William Pryce worked, but as she had just experienced, it had come back to bite her.

The bond William and I had formed was not at all what she had expected. I had longed to escape her controlling grasp and William, formerly widowed and childless, had needed an heir he could trust. The arrangement was perfect.

And now, with William stepping in as my manager, he was about to give me control of my own career, and life, and for that I was ever grateful. He promised counsel and advice, but I would make my own decisions regarding my roles, my productions, and how my theater was run. With his guidance I had hired Thomas Blackthorn, a sage veteran of theater and actor management, to co-manage my affairs, as William was often traveling. Mr. Blackthorn also handled the bulk of the everyday business minutia, but I had the last word on everything. I was finally mistress of my own destiny.

And I knew my mother would never accept it.

I shook off my anxiety in regards to her persistence, and the unsettling feeling Mr. Hughley had produced in me, and was determined to enjoy my fellow castmates in their revelry.

I walked back into the greenroom and was greeted with boisterous frivolity and laughter.

Maurice was drinking down an entire bottle of champagne, no longer bothering to use a glass. A large cake, which sat on a round table near the center of the room, which was once a decorated piece of glory, was now unrecognizable as the cast members had taken to it with a cake knife, but not in a neat and orderly way. It toppled to one side and crumbs had fallen everywhere.

Used tableware was left on chairs, and a pile of plates was stacked on one of the two divans. One of the actresses had uncorked another bottle and was sloppily pouring champagne into outstretched coupes just as Mrs. Ellen Greer, one of the cleaning staff, entered the room behind me.

"For Heaven's sake," she muttered under her breath. She stood beside me, her hands on her hips, one of them holding a feather duster comprised of ruddy brown ostrich feathers. Mrs.

Greer was a rather severe looking woman with a long face, pointed chin, and small, ice-blue eyes.

Her demeanor toward me had been quite frosty of late. Her husband, John, had also been in my employ as a stage hand. But seeing as he'd rather spend time in gambling halls than come to work, I had to fire him. Ever since, Mrs. Greer could scarcely contain her contempt for me, even though I kept her on because they clearly needed the money.

"And, I was to go home early tonight," she continued with a scowl.

I was taken aback at her comment. When she took the job, she knew she, or whomever was scheduled to clean, would be here late on performance nights. Her insolence was becoming tiresome.

"Pardon me?" I gave her a pointed look.

She huffed. "I'll never get home at this rate."

Her sour attitude oozed off of her, raising my ire. I had half a mind to dismiss her right then and there, but I controlled myself.

"You will get home, Mrs. Greer," I countered, "just not as early as you would like."

"Early in the morning you mean."

The cheek! I wanted to tell her that she would stay as long as I required, but after just going round with my mother, didn't have the energy.

"The cast will not remain much longer as they have gone through almost all of the champagne. For now, you may go to my dressing room and tidy up, there."

"Yes, Mrs. Pryce." Her voice had a coldness to it that made me shiver. She turned on her heel and left the green room.

"Everything all right?" Cordelia made her way over to me.

"Yes," I drew out. "That woman, Mrs. Greer, is an impudent one."

"I believe she has a lot to contend with, with that husband of hers."

I scoffed. "You'd think she'd be grateful that she still has her position. She just spoke to me as if I were nothing but a fellow maid—and one beneath her I might add."

"Oh, well—" Cordelia's gaze shifted from mine and she pulled her lower lip between her teeth. She looked mildly uncomfortable.

"What is it?" I asked.

"I don't think she likes you," she said softly.

"Well that's obvious. I fired her husband." A sinking feeling hit my stomach. I couldn't bear to be disliked.

"I mean—even before that. She thinks you're a snob."

"A snob? What right does she have to think that? I've done her a favor. I've given her work."

In fact, I was quite magnanimous will all of my employees.

"It's not you, Arabella. Not really. It's . . . well, it's the fact that you have money. I overheard her talking with Rebecca. She said something to the effect that no person should have so much money—that it makes them hateful."

My mouth dropped open. "My goodness! How can a person's bank account have anything to do with their character?"

She shrugged. "It's silly. And it's her problem, not yours. People love you—you know that."

"And Rebecca? Does she feel the same way? What did she say about me?" My fears and insecurities reared their ugly heads, and I knew I sounded desperate and defensive, but I couldn't help it.

"Oh no. Rebecca defended you. Said you were a good person. She is grateful for the job, Arabella—with her Althea so sick and all."

I took in a deep breath and let it out slowly, trying to breathe out the swirl of butterflies in my belly. Cordelia, practical and pragmatic in every way, never tried to patronize me.

"And you? Do you think I'm a snob?"

She pulled her upper lip between her teeth, and blinked at me. "I think you could do with a little more . . . patience with people."

I sighed. Cordelia always spoke the truth, as she saw it, and I knew she was right, much as I didn't want to admit it. I made a mental note to try to do as she'd suggested.

"Don't worry about Mrs. Greer," she went on. "She is the type of person who will always find something to be unhappy about. It is kind of you to keep her on."

I reached out and took her hand, grateful that she always could seem to calm me. "Thank you."

"Now," she said, smiling. "Let's get a glass of that champagne before it's all gone!"

We stayed with the cast and crew till well after one o'clock in the morning. As they began to trickle away in search of another party and more libations, Cordelia and I retired to my dressing room to gather our things before calling a cab to go home. William had long ago left to go to his club, and I was certain my mother had grown tired of waiting for me and had left as well.

When we opened the door, my assumption had been right. My mother was gone, and no one remained in the dressing room except for Bijou, who was peacefully sleeping on her little velvet bed. I flopped into the arm chair that was sitting next to my vanity.

"What a night!" I said.

"You were brilliant, Arabella. As usual."

I smiled with gratification.

"It smells wonderful in here," Cordelia said sniffing the air. "What is it?"

I shrugged a shoulder, straining to check my face in the full length mirror that was positioned next to the chair. "I don't smell it."

"Hmm." She said. "And, what is this?" she asked. I turned to look at her and she was pointing to something on my vanity. It was a black hat with a plume of black ostrich feathers adorning it. "Is it yours?"

"No. It looks like—"

"A mourning hat." She finished for me.

"What is it doing there?" I got up from the chair and went to the vanity. There were several bouquets of flowers and some odd trinkets littering the top of it. Gifts from fans. The funeral hat was definitely unusual. Next to it was a bottle of Florida Water. The elixir was a popular fragrance worn by both men and women. I had never used it myself. I lifted the hat to find the small bronze and burl walnut jewelry box in which I'd kept my ring, and some other jewelry. I was surprised to see it sitting there, because I usually kept it in the drawer of the vanity, out of sight. On top of the box was a note that read: "Condolences."

I swallowed at the ominous nature of the word. I opened the box and the earth shifted beneath my feet.

"Oh no!" I cried. My heart pounded against my ribs so hard I could barely breathe.

"What is it?" Cordelia came over to me.

My hand shook as I raised it to my mouth. Tears stung at the back of my eyes, burning my nasal passages.

"My ring! My ring is gone."

CHAPTER 3

"Gone? What do you mean gone?" Cordelia peered into the box.

Strangely enough, a bracelet William had given me was still there, along with a gold locket necklace in which I carried a photograph of my father.

"And, look." I handed her the note and her face paled.

Cordelia sucked in a breath. "Oh dear. What does this mean? Condolences for what? Or whom?"

"But, my ring!" I nearly wailed. I know it might seem strange that I was more worried about my ring than the threat of death, but losing my ring was like a death. Without it, everything would change.

"Did you put it back when you came off stage?" she asked, familiar with my habit.

A lump had formed in my throat. That and the panic in my chest both threatened to strangle me.

"No. I forgot and went directly to the greenroom. I gave it to Rebecca to put it away. She knows where I keep the box hidden."

"Are you sure you put the box back after you'd taken the ring for your performance?"

"I could have sworn I did—but, I was pretty nervous, like I always am on opening night."

"Perhaps Rebecca still has the ring," Cordelia said, trying to assert some positivity. "Maybe she forgot to put the ring in the box? And she might have seen who delivered the hat. Is she still here?"

"I doubt it. She said she had to get home to her girls."

"Well, then, maybe in her hurry to leave she forgot to come back to your dressing room, entirely."

"But, Bijou is here," I said, pointing to the little puppy. "I asked Rebecca to bring her to her bed. She must have been here."

"It's late," Cordelia reasoned. "We'll talk to her tomorrow."

I shook my head, my anxiety reaching a crescendo. "I don't know what will become of me if I don't find that ring."

A memory resurfaced.

The memory of my father leaving us. He'd come home very early one morning, which was not uncommon. He often came home in the wee hours, smelling of whiskey and occasionally the fragrance of a woman's perfume, much to my mother's displeasure. This particular morning had been no different in that regard, but *he* was different. Exuberant.

He'd told us he'd found a benefactress.

"She's a very wealthy woman." He had said. "She believes in my poetry, and she has connections with a publisher. Millicent, this is it! This is what I have been waiting for!"

My mother's face hardened. "A woman."

It seemed women loved my father with his golden mane of wavy hair and leonine yellow eyes. I couldn't blame them. In my ten-year-old heart, he was the most wonderful man in the world.

"Yes, yes, a woman. But it's not like that." He waved a hand in the air in an attempt to dismiss her worries, but I knew it wouldn't. "I leave for France tomorrow," he'd said. "That's where the publisher is. Hélène wants me to go with her to meet him."

I still remembered the panic I'd felt at the declaration. He was leaving me alone with my mother. She often belittled me, or made me feel that I never measured up. With him, I felt accepted. Whole. I needed him to counterbalance those uncomfortable feelings. Which he always did.

Mother had stormed into the bedroom, slamming the door.

Father sighed. "It's never enough," he said, shaking his head. "Whatever I do, it is never enough."

He rose wearily from the chair and took me under the arms, lifting me to his chest. I wrapped my legs around his waist and we held each other tight for a long time. In his embrace I felt safe, secure, and loved. But when he set me down, I knew in my heart I would never feel that embrace again.

He walked out of our flat, and never returned.

At first, we both received letters, and poetry from him, and some money. But then it all came less and less frequently. Within two years of his absence I had become a stage phenom, and had started to make decent money. My mother had worked hard to secure me roles throughout London's theater district.

One of the last letters I had received from my father, on my twelfth birthday, came with a small parcel. It was the Forget-Me-Not ring.

"My dearest Arabella, my sweet little Bijou,

I write to wish you the happiest of birthdays, and to bestow upon you this lovely ring. It will bring you luck, and success, like I have enjoyed. I've heard you are making quite a splash in the theater, darling, and I am so proud of you. Wear this ring and think of me.

Forever yours, Father.

And, he had been right. From that day on I wore the ring for every performance, and my success had been monumental, far eclipsing his, to my mother's delight.

But now that the ring was gone, what would become of me? I knew nothing but my art. It was my heart, my breath, my life. Without the ring that lifeforce would be gone, and I would be as I had always feared I would be: Worthless.

I sucked in a breath, my pulse raging through my ears.

"Perhaps that was what the condolences are for," I said under my breath.

"What?" Cordelia asked.

"My career. What if whomever took my ring knew exactly what it meant to me? Oh, Cordelia. What am I to do?"

She reached out and took my hand. "I know you're upset, but please try to calm yourself. We might ask Mrs. Greer," Cordelia said, shaking me from my terror. "She might have seen something. Didn't she come in here to clean earlier?"

"Yes," I said sullenly.

"Look." She bent down and picked up a feather. It was an ostrich feather, but it had been clipped short. It was brown, not black like the feathers in the funeral hat. "I wonder where this came from? Perhaps it's a clue. I'm going to look for Mrs. Greer. I saw her heading toward the green room."

Still stunned at my misfortune, I waved her away. Despondent, I sank down on the Queen Anne style settee, and Bijou jumped up and onto my lap to offer what comfort she could.

CHAPTER 4

Heartbroken and exhausted, I leaned my head against the back of the settee and closed my eyes. What had happened to the ring? I hoped upon hope that Rebecca still had it in her possession. But what about the funeral hat and cryptic condolences?

"I'm sorry to see you so upset." A soft, woman's voice whispered in my ear and a coolness wrapped itself around me, sending a shiver down my spine.

My eyes sprang open to find a semi-transparent figure of a woman sitting next to me. I gasped in surprise.

"Don't be afraid, my dear. I won't harm you."

I jumped up, knocking poor Bijou to the ground. Luckily, she landed on her feet.

"Who are you? What—are you?"

But then I knew, and a different kind of terror struck my heart. She was a ghost.

My fear did not stem from the fact that she was an otherworldly spirit, but it came from the reality that something in me had broken. Perhaps with the loss of the ring. I had long ago learned to shut myself off from this type of phenomenon, so why was I experiencing this now?

"My name is Leticia Crookshank. It's a pleasure to meet you, Arabella." Her voice had a velvety quality and the rapid pounding of my pulse slowed a fraction. Her attire was of popular fashion in the 1850's, some twenty years ago. Her plaid dress, with its lace collar, full bishop sleeves and wide hoopskirt showed off an impossibly narrow waist.

The first—and last, up to this point—ghost I had seen was in my childhood. My friend and playmate Oliver Shrewsbury, who had succumbed to influenza, had come to visit me while on a picnic with Mother and some of her friends. I had thought that Oliver had somehow recovered and come back to us. But when I had explained his visit to his parents later that day, I had realized my mistake.

My faux-pax had resulted in several visits to a friend of my mother's. A spiritualist. My mother had explained to me, and to her friend, that this type of sensitivity ran in the family. She herself did not possess the gift, but saw some of the painful repercussions for some of her relatives who did. One went mad young, and another had been accused of being a witch. Both had ended up in an asylum until their deaths. Afraid that I would fall prey to the same fate, she arranged for me to learn how to close myself off to my extra senses. It was an emotionally painful process, but it had been successful.

Until now.

"Why are you here?" I asked.

She smiled, causing the skin around her pale eyes to crinkle at the corners. She looked to be of a mature age when she died.

"I live here."

"For—for how long?"

William and I had owned the theater for four years, and I had never had even an inkling of her presence.

"Oh, many years. I died in 1853. Onstage. During a performance. It was my heart you see."

"I—I'm sorry," I stammered, not sure how to express condolences to a person who had passed from this realm.

She nodded in thanks. "I was never able to take my final curtain call—so I stay. It's my home. But, enough about me, you are distressed my dear. What's happened?"

Her voice was so tender and caring that it caused a swell of emotion to rise up inside of me. I let go a sob, and blubbered through my telling of what had happened.

"That ring means everything to me." I finished. I gathered myself together, embarrassed at my display. I rarely succumbed to tears. Not since I'd seen the spiritualist. That part of me had been cut off, too.

She reached out and laid a transparent hand on my shoulder. I could not feel the weight of it, but an icy coolness oozed down my arm.

"Did you see anything?" I asked. "Did you see who brought that?" I pointed to the funeral hat.

"No, I'm afraid not. I was in the theater—it's where I prefer to be. I came here when I sensed your unhappiness."

Bijou, who had been staring at the apparition the entire time, let out a squeaky little puppy bark.

"I just don't know what I'm going to do," I said, wiping the tears from my cheek with the back of my hand. "I've never performed without it."

When I looked over toward her again, she'd vanished.

Cordelia breezed into the room. "I couldn't find Mrs. Greer. Everyone is gone."

"Oh," I said, startled at her sudden appearance and feeling a bit like I'd been caught in the act of something dreadful. "Well, I cannot be without that ring. We must find it." I pulled up one of the cushions from the settee, looking under it.

She came over to me and took me by the elbow. "Tomorrow, Arabella. It's very late, and you are exhausted. You need to be fresh for your next performance. You must get some sleep."

My next performance. The night after tomorrow night. The thought squeezed the blood out of my heart, making my knees feel weak and watery. What would happen if I didn't find the ring by then? What if my performance was dull and lifeless and . . . flat?

Oh, how I had wished I'd had an understudy. Molly Dunn, the woman who had filled that role for me in the past and had been hired for this show, had taken another part—a leading role — at the last minute. She had claimed that I never let her have any stage time, and that her talent was going to waste. My pride, (or my insecurities about being upstaged), would someday be the end of me.

What if I failed?

I would never be able to bear the shame.

CHAPTER 5

The following day, Bijou and I arrived at the theater early in the morning. I usually never got there before ten o'clock, but I knew Rebecca often came in early. I wanted to see her as soon as possible. The rest of the company would be arriving at noon for a recap of last night's performance. We often did this during the first week of the show so that we might discuss and iron out any problems we had encountered on stage.

William had wanted to get to his office early as well, to tie up some loose ends before his trip to La Plata Springs, so we rode together in his carriage.

"I'd like to accompany you inside." He said. "That note of condolences was upsetting and I am concerned for your safety. And, I can help you look for the ring."

I laid my gloved hand on his cheek and looked into his bright brown eyes which shone with cleverness. "Thank you, darling, but I know you have important business to take care of before your journey. Rebecca should be here."

I had the sinking feeling that if the ring was indeed stolen, the threat was not meant for my physical body, but for my soul. This was personal. Deeply personal. Whomever did this did not mean to kill me. Just ruin me. And, I would not let that happen.

"I do have a meeting in an hour—and really mustn't be late," he said. "But I can spend a little while with you, to see that all is safe inside before I go."

I smiled at him, touched that he had offered to help and that he was concerned for my wellbeing.

"All right," I agreed. "I'd like the company."

Bijou licked my chin. "Aside from Bijou, of course." I chuckled.

And I would like William's company. The truth of the matter was that my husband and I spent very little time together. When he was at home, it seemed we drifted in and out of our Fifth Avenue mansion without seeing each other for days.

We alighted from the carriage and entered through the back door in the alley way. The hallway that led to the interior of the theater was dark, but I knew the catacombs of the building so well I could have been blindfolded and still been able to get around easily.

"I'll go first," he said. "To make sure no one is lurking around."

He went ahead of me and I hung back. I set Bijou on the ground and she perused the place with her nose.

Something glowing in the darkness stopped me short. Bijou must have seen it too, because she started barking.

"Bijou, shush!" I whispered and picked her up.

"You're here early," a soft voice permeated the air. I narrowed my eyes to see better. The milky apparition moved closer and I was soon enveloped in a cool mist.

"Miss Crookshank?"

Bijou growled.

"It is." She slowly gave a nod of her head.

"I'm here to look for the ring," I said. "With my husband."

My pulse quickened, afraid that William might hear me speaking to someone that supposedly wasn't there. For if he, or anyone, knew I could see and communicate with ghosts . . .

"My husband doesn't know about my . . . abilities. He mustn't see me talking with you. And, he mustn't see you, either. It would complicate things greatly for me. Please."

"I will not reveal myself to him. Besides, I sense that his barriers are nearly impenetrable. It would be quite taxing for me to do so. I will stay out of his view, I promise."

I nodded, sensing her sincerity. I knew she meant me no harm.

"Did you happen upon the ring while I was gone?" I asked her.

"No, I'm afraid not, my dear."

"Is Rebecca, my dresser, here?"

Leticia gave a nod of her head. "Yes, she arrived a few minutes ago."

"Arabella!" William called out. "It's all right. You can come through. Did I hear Bijou barking?"

Miss Crookshank winked at me and then vanished.

"Yes. She must have seen a mouse." I said by way of explanation. "Rebecca is here and I'd like to—"

A bewildered expression crossed his features. "How do you know that?"

"Oh, well. She usually arrives early." I said, hoping the answer was satisfactory. How could I tell him I'd heard it from a ghost?

"She's probably in the wardrobe room." I finished and led the way.

She was indeed there.

"Good morning, Mrs. Pryce," she said with some surprise. "You are here early." Her gaze shifted to William. "Mr. Pryce," she nodded.

"Morning," he said and then turned to me. "Well darling, now that I know you are not alone, I will go. I'm meeting Tisdale this morning." He indicated with a tilt of his head for me to follow him out of the room. I was impatient to query Rebecca, but I supposed it could wait a few minutes.

"Mr. Tisdale you say?" I asked. "Your lawyer?"

"Yes, I might as well take advantage of the time I am here to take care of some legal matters. It's time I change my will, as we have discussed. You, my darling, will get everything when I die."

I smiled. That had been the arrangement we had agreed upon when we married, but William had been so busy since then that he hadn't had time to do it. I was grateful that he was tending to this matter once and for all. I would never be dependent upon another person again. Including my mother.

"You really must come with me to Colorado to stay at The Arabella sometime. You will love it darling! After all, it will be yours someday. I'd like for you to see how we run things out there."

I tried to keep my smile from fading. While it was flattering that he'd named his prized project after me, and was bequeathing it to me, the last thing I wanted to do was to go there. I had no interest whatsoever in the running of a hotel.

"Of course, dear," I said, trying to drum up some enthusiasm.

"And, I am also finalizing the contract that makes Blackthorn your theater director, and co-manager of your career, along with me, of course."

"Thank you, darling." I planted a kiss on his cheek. A scuffling noise down the darkened hallway startled the both of us, but it only turned out to be Bijou. She scampered toward us but then turned and looked back from whence she'd come. I wondered if Miss Crookshank had appeared again.

"Must be the mouse," William mused.

"Here, Bijou," I said. She ran toward me.

"Be careful my dear," William warned.

I bid him goodbye and re-entered the wardrobe room.

"It's nice to see your husband," Rebecca said. "He doesn't come here often."

"No—no, he doesn't. Rebecca, do you still have my ring?" I didn't want to tarry over conversation.

She blinked at the question. "Your ring? No—no ma'am. I set it in the jewelry box, just like you asked."

"Did you put the box back into the drawer?"

She hesitated. "I—I think so."

I let out an exasperated sigh. "The jewelry box was on the vanity, and the ring is not there. It's gone."

She stared at me blankly.

"You're sure you left it in the jewelry box?" I pressed.

"Yes ma'am." This time, her voice had an edge to it.

"Was the funeral hat there? Had it been placed on the jewelry box?"

She gave me a quizzical look and I explained.

"No," she shook her head. "I did not see a hat. There were some other items on the vanity—gifts."

"Yes, yes," I sighed. "Thank you, Rebecca."

I wanted to believe Rebecca. And did, for the most part, but I knew she needed money. Her little Althea was sickly and needed medical care. Her eldest daughter quit school to care for her while Rebecca worked. A tidy sum for the sale of the ring would be most welcomed in the Poitier household. But if she was lying about the ring, was she lying about the hat?

My chest tightened. What did it all mean?

With Bijou on my heels, I made my way to the stage. I had little hope of finding it there, but was determined to scour the entire building. My search felt a bit futile, as the ring had so clearly been taken, but I had to do something. What if the thief had unknowingly dropped it? Or what if they had hidden it? I needed to at least try. I started by looking under and around every piece of furniture and prop of the set.

It suddenly seemed silly to pin my entire future on a ring. I was, and, thanks to William, always would be, a very wealthy woman but the unsettling threat of that particular item having some kind of power over my talent wouldn't let me go. Would having money help if I could not succeed at my art? The thing that gave my life meaning?

In my heart of hearts I knew that it wouldn't.

I perused the stage one more time and was just about to give up, when a noise behind me startled me. I whirled around to see my mother, standing there like she had been watching me for some time.

"And what will become of me?" She said.

Bijou, startled as well, barked, but when she recognized my mother, she ran up to her and raised herself on her hind legs for a pat on the head. My mother ignored her.

"Mother! You scared the life out of me." I pressed a hand to my chest to still my racing heartbeat. "What are you doing here so early?"

"I went to your dressing room to speak with you. One of the maids at the mansion, the homely one, told me you'd come to the theater." She primly folded her hands at her waist. Clasped within them was a folded, ostrich feather fan. The one she always carried with her of late to soothe the waves of heat that often overcame her. She was experiencing the change and was often quite uncomfortable.

"Oh," I said, catching my breath. "I'm rather busy at the moment. My ring has gone missing. The one father gave me. You haven't seen it have you?"

She smirked. "No. Not since Rebecca deposited it in your jewelry box. Shortly after we spoke."

"I see." So Rebecca had not taken the ring. I should have known better. She was an honest woman.

"How long were you in my dressing room waiting for me last night? Did anyone come in? There were some gifts left there for me."

She lifted a shoulder. "Yes. I—I left for a moment to, well, to go to the powder room. The gifts were there when I returned," she flipped open the fan and waved it near her face. She must have been experiencing a surge of heat. One of the feathers dislodged itself and floated to the stage. I stared at it. It was the same color as the one that Cordelia found on the dressing room floor.

"Did you see the funeral hat?"

Her gaze flitted away from mine. "I saw the hat," she said. "I wondered who had died. Or who is going to die. Maybe that and your missing ring are omens of something ill to come."

I knew she was trying to bring out my insecurities. My mother had always been jealous of my former relationship with my father, and had often punished me for it. When I'd received the ring in the post, she didn't speak to me for two days.

I stiffened at her attempt to unsettle me further. "I have to find it. Before the performance Sunday night."

She gave me a sinister smile. "You are far too superstitious about that ring, dear."

I narrowed my eyes at her, suddenly remembering that once, a few years after I'd received the gift from my father, we'd gotten into a terrible row about it. She insisted I go on stage without the ring. She wanted to prove that I could still be brilliant without it, but I had refused. It was one of the only times I had ever stood up to her as a young girl.

I blew out a breath in exasperation. "Is there something you wanted, Mother?"

Her mouth straightened to a thin line. "So, my suspicions were correct. It's final is it? You discarding me into the street like some old rubbish? Without me, you'd be nothing, Arabella."

I blinked, not knowing what to say. I knew she had an inkling of our plans, but then she must have overheard my conversation with William confirming them. I recalled the noise in the hallway that we had heard, and Bijou's behavior, like she'd seen something.

I swallowed. The dreaded moment had come. "I—I wanted to tell you myself. I didn't mean for you to find out this way."

She raised her chin and her eyes took on a hardness that took my breath away.

"You'll fail, Arabella. I made you who you are. I sacrificed all those years to make you a star. And this is how you repay me?"

"Mother—I—I need some independence. I'm a grown woman. I need to make my way on my own. I will still take care of you."

"Take care of me?" She scoffed. "You can't even take care of yourself. You are replacing me with William and that theater manager—you'll still be dependent. You can't manage your career. You have no head for business, Arabella. You'll still be just a pretty song bird in a gilded cage."

My teeth clenched together so hard my jaw ached. How dare she speak to me this way. "That's not what William thinks," I retorted. "He thinks me quite capable. Why else would he leave everything to me? Even his hotel in Colorado."

Thunderclouds flitted across her face.

And then it dawned on me. If she somehow knew what was coming, she could have taken the ring, to punish me.

"Did you take the ring, Mother? Is this your way of exercising some kind of control over me? Do you want me to fail? And the hat? Were you expressing your condolences for my career—seeing as you think I'll fail without you."

Her mouth dropped open and then quickly snapped shut, hardening into a frown.

"Why would I want that worthless bauble?"

"It's not worthless, Mother. It is made with diamonds."

Her frown eased, giving way to a smirk. "It's paste. I'm sure of it."

"I don't care about its monetary value," I said. "It still means everything to me and you know it. You are punishing me for taking control of my own life."

She straightened her spine and closed her feathered fan with an angry click. "I don't need to steal that damn ring to punish you. By firing me, you are doing that yourself. You might want to check with that cheeky cleaning woman. She came to your dressing room last night. I found her there after I'd gone to the powder room."

She stalked off, her back rigid and the sound of her heels echoing through the theater.

If she'd taken the ring, what did she intend to do with it? Sell it? She would no longer be making money as my manager.

Perhaps she thought I would cut her out altogether. If I weren't so angry at her at the moment, I would have called her back to tell her that I had no intention of severing her allowance. She was my mother, after all. And she had made sure we had survived all those years ago. For that I was grateful.

If what she'd said was true about the diamonds not being real, it would indeed be worthless. In that case, if she took the ring it was more likely she would hold onto it. As a reminder and symbol of her power over me. I would find a way to search her room at the mansion as soon as I got home.

But first, I needed to speak with Mrs. Greer.

CHAPTER 6

It was half-past nine o'clock, and Mrs. Greer would not be here until ten. It wouldn't surprise me if she turned up late, having been here for so long last night. I regretted chastising her. I should have let her go home. What harm would it have done to let her get a good night's rest and then clean up in the morning when she was refreshed?

I went to my dressing room to look for the ring there again and think. Bijou went first to her water dish, and then curled up in her bed.

I sat down at my vanity, perusing the items left there. My eye was drawn to the bottle of Florida water. It was beautiful. Its long neck was wrapped in gold foil and the label was intricately decorated with floral wreathes, birds, and butterflies in an intricate Victorian motif.

Less appealing was the sight of the funeral hat. The design was pleasing, with a generous spray of black ostrich plumes gracing its crown, but the fact that it was there was disconcerting. If someone wanted to gift me with a hat, why not give me one in a more desirable color?

But no, there had also been the note. This was a warning. Or a threat.

My mother came to mind again. Would she really threaten death upon me, or someone close to me?

A sudden coolness wafted over my right side. Bijou had woken up and began to bark. I turned my head to see Miss Crookshank's ethereal, transparent form sitting on the settee.

"Oh, hello," I said, not warmly I fear. I did not want to engage in conversation at the moment, I wanted to think. "Bijou, be quiet."

The little urchin emitted a low growl and then was silent.

"Any luck?" Miss Crookshank asked.

"No. I'm waiting to speak with Mrs. Greer. Did you see her last night? Do you know how late she stayed?"

"The last I saw of her, she was up on the catwalk during the party."

"The catwalk?" I asked, somewhat surprised.

"She was dusting up there—although I'm not sure why. It vexed me because I had to stay out of sight, and the rafters are my favorite place to be. I find it so restful there."

"Well, she is very thorough," I said. "And I've asked her to keep things clean up there, you know, to help prevent the possibility of a fire."

Mr. Potter, the Rigger, kept a few oil lanterns up on the catwalk. Any extraneous debris might cause trouble.

"I don't know how long she stayed after the party," Miss Crookshank finished. "Do you think she stole your ring? Is she a suspect?"

I sighed. "I don't know. She's been quite angry with me since I had to let her husband go. She could have taken it in revenge. Oh, I don't know who to trust—except William and Cordelia, of course. And . . . You. You didn't—"

"I did not," she said, a little affronted. "I cannot possess a physical object. Nor move one. But, what about that young man? Your leading man? Maurice is it?"

"Maurice? Do you know something?"

"I saw him near your dressing room. With another man—the one who plays Friar Tuck."

"Really. When was this?"

"During the party. They might have been going to his dressing room—it is next door to yours. But, he seemed angry—and quite drunk."

I sighed. "He was. Both." I told her about not renewing his contract for the tour.

"Ah." She nodded.

"Do you think he stole the ring?" I asked.

She shrugged, but didn't verbalize an answer.

"If he did, then what about the funeral hat? He'd only just found out about our plans to exclude him from the tour. He didn't have time to go out and buy one. And, Mrs. Greer could not afford it. Where would either one of them have obtained it?"

"The costume room?" she said.

"Yes. Of course," I said, musing on this new possibility. Both Maurice and Mrs. Greer could have been motivated by revenge to take the ring. Both knew I always wore it on stage. Maurice and I had even discussed our lucky talismans—my ring and his hat. And, in his case, at least, the funeral hat could have been a sick joke. He was prone to pranks.

The dressing room door opened and Miss Crookshank vanished.

It was Mrs. Greer with her cleaning cart. Her feather duster was clutched in her hand—as usual.

"Oh! I didn't think you'd been in so early, ma'am. I'll just—" She turned to leave, but I stopped her.

"Wait, Mrs. Greer. I'd like to speak with you."

Her face went sour. "What is it, ma'am?"

"Did you see anyone in here after the performance? During the party? Perhaps when you came here to tidy up?"

"Only your mother," she said with a sneer. "Right rude she was to me. Told me not to come in here."

"Really . . . so you weren't in here at all last night?"

"No ma'am."

"Are you sure?"

She pulled her chin back and blinked at me. "She told me not to come in."

"But did you?" I repeated. "Perhaps when she'd gone to the powder room?"

"What are you getting at, ma'am?" Her eyes had gone stony, and her mouth twitched with anger.

I told her about the stolen ring, and pointed to the funeral hat. "Do you know anything about that? Was the hat here when you came to tidy up?"

"I don't know, ma'am," she said loudly, clearly annoyed with my questions. "I was told to leave."

"But did you leave?" I repeated.

"Are you saying I stole the ring, and left that?"

I didn't answer, but simply regarded her with interest, hoping she would say more.

Then she laughed, but it wasn't a pleasant laugh. "And where would I get that hat? Looks mighty expensive. Not all of us can afford such finery," she said with contempt. "'Specially as seein' that my John has no work."

And, there it was. She was furious with me for firing her husband—and, she did resent me for my money. I was about to chide her for her disrespect. In fact, I should have fired *her* for her impertinence, but I wanted to continue with my line of inquiry instead. "You could have obtained it from the costume room," I said, taking Miss Crookshank's point.

She set her fists on her plump hips and my gaze was drawn to the feather duster. "You've got a point there, don't you? I could have—but I didn't. And, I didn't take your ring, neither."

"If you weren't in here, why was there a feather—much like the one in your duster—found on the floor?"

She took in a deep breath through her nose, her mouth turning down with disdain. "I have no idea, ma'am," she said through gritted teeth. "And I resent the insinuation."

"You resent everything about me, don't you?" I said quietly. I realized I was pushing pretty hard—and I had let my emotions get in front of me. I couldn't abide not being liked, or at least respected. It tore at my soul. I did have half a mind to fire her, to be rid of her, but if I did that, I might not get to the truth about the ring. I needed everyone to stay put until it was found.

She didn't answer my question, which spoke volumes.

"You can go, Mrs. Greer. You can clean up in here, later."

She threw her feather duster down on her cart, and left me with a hateful glare in her eyes.

CHAPTER 7

I was fairly convinced that Mrs. Greer seemed a likely culprit, but I couldn't be absolutely sure. I needed to leave no stone unturned.

By this time, I only had less than an hour to continue my search before the other cast members arrived for our meeting. I looked throughout the theater for the ring. I even searched the large dressing room shared by several of the cast members, and the private dressing room of my leading man.

His room was an unholy mess with clothing strewn about. Several liquor bottles and dirty glasses cluttered his vanity. Food was left rotting on plates on a table, and there was even one plate left on the floor that Bijou happily discovered.

"Bijou, don't eat that!" I shooed her away and set the plate back on the table out of her reach. When I turned back around, she had discovered his Robin Hood hat, which was also on the floor, and picked it up in her teeth. She waddled over to me.

"You'd better put that down, little girl. Maurice would not appreciate teeth marks in his hat."

I took it from her and was about to hang it up on a peg on the wall when something about it caught my notice. I studied the feather that was tucked into the hat band. Hadn't there been two of them before? Perhaps he had been in my dressing room as Miss Crookshank had suggested—taking my ring—and one of them had fallen from the hat?

I put the hat back on the peg and searched every nook and cranny of the room, trying my best to put everything back as I had found it, but uncovered nothing else of interest.

However, my fears that Maurice had wanted to punish me for not including him in the tour were confirmed when he did not show up for our cast meeting. I tried to assure myself with the fact that this had happened before, when he'd spent the night out on the town until late into the morning, but on this day, it gave me more cause for alarm than usual. What if he had been so angry about the tour that he'd decided to leave the show? And took my ring with him?

The rest of the cast members conducted our review without him. Cordelia, as usual, made a record of all the items to be addressed, which were pleasantly very few. Our meeting was followed up with a quick rehearsal with Maurice's understudy, Theodore, standing in for him. He was a sturdy looking fellow, not as handsome as Maurice, and not quite as charming either, but he was solid, dependable, and his talent was blossoming. Despite that, the rehearsal, suffice it to say, was a disaster.

But not due to poor performance on anyone else's part, only my own. I couldn't seem to get my lines right. I stumbled on my words, I missed cues from my fellow actors, and at times I couldn't remember my lines at all.

After the rehearsal, I asked Jacob Blythe, the man who played Friar Tuck, to stay behind. He was a corpulent fellow, with a bald head and fleshy jowls, who fit the part exceedingly well.

"Jacob, do you know where Maurice is?" I asked him.

He let out a snort. "I'm pretty sure he's still knocked out cold from last night's party. He really tied one on."

I chuckled in agreement. "Yes, I'm sure that's it. But, Jacob, did you happen to see him near my dressing room last night?"

He blinked in confusion at my rapid change of subject. "*Your* dressing room?"

"Yes." I didn't elaborate, waiting for him to offer what he would.

"He went to *his* dressing room. Or, rather, I brought him there to help him get changed out of his costume. The man didn't know up from down."

"Was he angry?" I asked.

He scoffed. "Maurice always gets moody when he drinks."

"What did you do after you helped him change his clothes?"

"We went back to the party. Stayed for a while, but he'd passed out in a chair, so I poured him into a cab and sent him home."

So Maurice had not been in my dressing room. At least, not with Jacob.

"I see. Thank you, Jacob. By the way, would you do me a favor?" I asked him.

"Sure," he said with a nod.

"Something has gone missing from my dressing room. It was my ring."

His eyebrows shot up, wrinkling his broad forehead. "Your lucky ring?"

"Yes."

"Oh, my. I'm very sorry, Arabella."

"Thank you. Would you please let the rest of the cast and crew know about it? And, tell them I am offering a generous reward to anyone who finds it?" It was my hope that Mrs. Greer, or Maurice, or whomever might have taken it, would be tempted by the offer of a reward to find their conscience again and return it.

"Of course." He said.

I sent him on his way, hoping my declaration would bear fruit.

Back in my dressing room, Cordelia implored me to go home

and rest my voice for tomorrow's production. I agreed, and we both set out in the carriage for the mansion.

But once there, I but could not rest. Instead, I took advantage of the fact that my mother had gone shopping—something that would inevitably take her all day—and went to her room to search for the ring. Unfortunately, I was interrupted by the maid and had to leave my search till a later time.

Unable to settle myself at home, I went back to the theater taking Cordelia and Bijou with me. I wanted to be there in case the ring miraculously turned up. Ignoring Cordelia's pleas that I stay silent for the sake of my voice, I questioned everyone, to no avail.

Later that afternoon, exhausted and frustrated by my unsuccessful inquiries, I made my way slowly to the stage and stood under the proscenium arch looking out into the empty house. Where once before, this was the place where I stood to take my final bow, receive my accolades and the adoration I so craved, it was now a place filled with dread. I could not perform without the ring. Based upon my earlier rehearsal, it would prove to be a horror.

The sound of footsteps coming across the stage caught my attention.

It was William, which was strange. He rarely came to the theater, except on opening night when he happened to be in town, and today he had been here twice.

"You're back," I said. "This is a nice surprise."

A look of confusion crossed over his features. "But, I received a note at the club saying I was needed at the theater. I assumed it was from you.."

Now, it was my turn to be confused. "A note? I didn't send a note."

"Well, I am here, now. Shall I escort you home?"

I wondered if Cordelia, concerned about my frantic and obsessive state of mind, had sent for him for this very reason—

to get me home again to rest. It would definitely be in character for her to do so.

I crossed the stage and went to the sofa. I plopped down in despair. "I've had no luck finding the ring."

"It is of no consequence, Arabella. I'll buy you a new one."

My mouth dropped open in chagrin. "The ring had meaning, William. It cannot be replaced."

He shrugged. "It's just a *thing*. This delusion that somehow the ring makes you who you are as an actress is not rational, darling."

I slammed my hands down on the sofa, irritated at his pragmatism. "Don't speak to me about rationality, William. You just don't understand!"

"Excuse me, Mrs. Pryce?" Mrs. Greer had come onto the stage, sans her cart, working her hands at her waist, her face twisted with worry.

"What is it?" I snapped. My frustration with William's lack of regard for my feelings spilled over to her.

Mrs. Greer's gaze flitted to William and then back to me. "I just wanted to apologize—for earlier. I shouldn't have spoken to you so."

Something from above cracked. I looked up to see that a backdrop rigging had come loose and was hurtling to the floor. I jumped to my feet and flung myself at William to knock him out of the way, and we both pitched to the ground. The rigging fell with a loud boom, landing right alongside us. A cloud of dust exploded into the air.

Bijou, who had quickly jumped away, began barking furiously. William groaned in pain and clutched at his chest.

The crash still ringing in my ears, I managed to sit up. Bijou quieted and scuttled over to me.

"William! William, are you hurt?"

He gasped for air. "I—I—"

I glanced at the rigging again and my stomach twisted. Sprawled beneath it was poor Mrs. Greer.

"Good Heavens!" Cordelia came rushing onto the stage. "Mrs. Greer!"

She ran across the stage and then attempted to lift the rigging, but she was a small woman, and the contraption was far too heavy.

I struggled to my feet to help, but the thing wouldn't budge.

Cordelia reached down and pressed her fingers to Mrs. Greer's throat, looking for a pulse.

"Is she dead?" I cried,

"No. Just unconscious."

William groaned again.

"Mr. Pryce, are you all right?" Cordelia asked him.

He gasped again and this time took in a big gulp of air. "Yes, Yes, I believe so," he said, holding up a hand. Sitting up he grimaced. His handsome face had gone quite gray. "I think I'm fine. Just got the wind knocked out of me."

"I'm so sorry, darling," I said. "I—"

"Dear God." He looked over at the prostrate body of Mrs. Greer, partially buried under the backdrop.

"We need to get that rigging off of her," I said. "It's too heavy for us."

William started to get to his feet to help.

"No," I said. "You catch your breath." He'd said he was all right, but I wanted to make sure.

"Cordelia, find Mr. Potter." I said.

Without another word, she fled backstage.

I helped William up and got him to the sofa. I then went to Mrs. Greer. She groaned, slowly gaining consciousness.

"Mrs. Greer?" I queried. "Mrs. Greer, it's Arabella."

"My leg," she croaked.

"Stay still. Someone is coming to help."

From the corner of my eye, I saw a shadowy figure in the wings.

"Mr. Potter?" I called out.

To my surprise, Maurice stepped into the light. "What's happened here?"

"Maurice! Come help me get this rigging off of Mrs. Greer."

He came over just as Mr. Potter and Cordelia came onto the stage. Together, we lifted the contraption, freeing the poor woman. She wailed in pain.

"My leg!"

The sound of rushing footsteps in the house drew my attention. Theodore was running down the aisle toward the stage.

"What happened? I heard a loud crash."

"It's Mrs. Greer. The rigging fell on her," I said. "I think her leg is broken. Could you and Maurice take her to the hospital?"

Theodore nodded. "I'll fetch a coach." He ran back up the aisle and out of the theater. Within a few minutes he'd returned. Together, he and Maurice got her to her feet. Theodore lifted her into his arms, and they made their way off the stage. Maurice, usually loquacious at every turn, had remained oddly quiet. Could it have been shock? And, furthermore, what had he been doing in the wings?

"Mr. Potter," I said, indicating with a tilt of my head toward the catwalk. "Find out what happened up there."

"I'll go, too," Cordelia volunteered.

I made my way over to check on William. The color had returned to his face, and he looked quite restored. In a few minutes, we heard footsteps on the catwalk from above, and the sound of Cordelia and Mr. Potter's murmured voices. Then, Cordelia gasped.

"What is it?" I shouted up to them.

"Rope's been cut," Mr. Potter answered back.

William and I exchanged a glance. "It was deliberate," I said.

William nodded. "Someone wanted to see one, or both of us, dead."

"And Mrs. Greer got in the way," I added.

CHAPTER 8

"We need to send for the police," William said. "Potter, you go. I don't want to leave Arabella. Tell them we need assistance right away."

"Yes, sir." Mr. Potter finished stacking some of the debris in a pile.

I reached out and took hold of William's sleeve, pulling William closer to me. "What if it was him?" I whispered.

"Potter?" He whispered back, glancing over at him.

Cordelia shook her head. "He'd just arrived," she said. "He was entering the theater from the alleyway through the backstage door."

William nodded. "Right. Make haste, Potter."

The Rigger stood and then jogged away from us.

"You should go home, Arabella," William said. "I'll wait for the police. Cordelia, would you take her?"

I folded my arms across my chest. "I'm not leaving. I want to tell them about my ring. And, the funeral hat. I am convinced this is all related."

"Which means you are in danger, my dear." William insisted. "It's quite fortuitous that my trip was delayed. I would hate to think of you enduring this alone."

I jutted my chin out. "What if it is *you* who are in danger?" I countered. "I've been on this stage a few times today, and nothing like this happened until you arrived. And exactly why did you arrive? Because you thought I had summoned you. Someone sent you that note."

I turned to Cordelia. "Did you sent the note requesting that William come to see me?"

She shook her head. "No, I didn't."

"See," I said. "Whomever sent it wanted you here."

He let out an impatient breath. "You will not be persuaded to go home, I see."

I shook my head.

"Well, perhaps you should go to your dressing room, Arabella," Cordelia said. "You two will be safe there."

"But how will Mr. Potter and the police know where to find us?" I asked.

"I'll keep an eye out for them." Cordelia reached out and touched my arm. I was about to open my mouth in protest when she gave me that bossy look of hers that rarely showed itself.

"I'll be careful," she said.

Reluctantly, I let William lead me to my dressing room. He settled himself on the settee, and Bijou joined him. I paced the floor. We were both silent, caught up in our own thoughts until Cordelia pushed through the dressing room door about an hour later. Behind her was a uniformed officer and behind him a man in a dashing suit. It was Mr. Hughley.

Ugh! I did not have time for this.

"What are you doing here?" I snapped at him. Bijou, standing at my feet let out a menacing growl. Well, menacing for a little dog who stood only about a foot high.

"Detective Hughley at your service." He removed his hat, releasing the spring of his dark curls, and gave a short bow. His gaze traveled to William briefly, then returned to me. "And this is Officer Trent," he indicated with a tilt of his head toward the uniformed man.

"You're a detective?" I asked, somewhat harshly, not quite able to believe it.

"I am. I had just returned to the station to find your employee reporting a problem at the theater. I had to come see for myself. I understand there has been some kind of accident?" He stood with his hat in one hand, which he'd placed behind his back, and the other in his coat pocket.

"Someone tried to kill us," William cut in. "They got Mrs. Greer instead. She's alive, but badly injured."

"And someone has stolen my ring—and this was left on top of the jewelry box I keep it in." I pointed to the funeral hat. "Along with a note of 'condolences'. Whomever left this was warning us of what would happen. I thought it might have been Mrs. Greer, but then why would she have come out on stage the very moment—"

"Your ring?" Detective Hughley interrupted.

"Yes. You commented on it yourself, last night." I said.

"You know this man?" William asked, sounding a bit alarmed.

Detective Hughley directed his attention to William. "I, like so many others, am quite an adoring fan of Mrs. Pryce."

I flinched at his use of the word "adoring." It seemed inappropriate for the occasion.

William cleared his throat, clearly picking up on the same thing, but did not press. He had become accustomed to the attentions my public lavished on me, but I dare say, in the company of this handsome detective, he took particular notice.

Determined to refocus the conversation, I explained what had happened with the rigging.

"Show me," the detective said.

We all went back to the stage. Mr. Potter was there, examining the rigging and the backdrop attached to it, probably trying to determine if it was salvageable or not.

"How awful," the detective said. He squatted down next to the rigging, then rose again. He circled the broken contraption and then looked up into the rafters.

"And, you say the ropes were cut?"

"Yes, sir." Mr. Potter said. "Clean through. Although, they are frayed now on account of losing their tension. But I keep an eye on the ropes, sir, to make sure they aren't worn out. I just replaced these a couple of weeks ago."

"Could you or one of your crew have been careless?" Detective Hughley asked pointedly.

Mr. Potter's jaw tightened. "No, sir. I've been doing this kind of work for fifteen years. I know my ropes, I know my rigging. I make sure the others working with me do, too. All was intact."

"May I?" The detective pointed to the catwalk and then placed his hat back on his head.

Mr. Potter gave a quick nod and led him to the ladder backstage. I followed and started up the ladder behind them.

"Arabella!" William called out.

"I'll be fine," I said, not willing to listen to his warnings.

About half way up, I mistakenly looked down upon the stage, which seemed so very far away. My head spun. I briefly closed my eyes to get my bearings again, and continued until I reached the catwalk where Detective Hughley was waiting with an outstretched hand. I took it and he hauled me to the platform, pulling me closer to him than was comfortable. I quickly released his hand and avoided eye contact. In doing so I inadvertently looked up over his head and saw Miss Crookshank, primly sitting on one of the wooden beams that held the ceiling together.

I sucked in a breath and nearly choked. She pressed a finger to pursed lips, silently shushing me.

Detective Hughley examined the ropes, which indeed had frayed. "Hard to see that they were cleanly cut, Potter," he said, looking over at the rigger.

"But, sir, they were. I can assure you of that."

"Hmmm. Could have been defective," he said, doubtfully. "Perhaps they looked strong, but then . . ."

The expression on Mr. Potter's face darkened.

Nervous about her sudden appearance, I glanced up at my ghostly friend who was pointing to something near the winch that served to move the rigging up and down. There was something dark stuck in it. I made my way over.

It was leather. I pulled it away to find that it was a glove. A man's black leather glove made of fine kidskin. I noted something odd. The pinkie finger of the glove looked fat, like it was stuffed with something.

"Look!" I exclaimed. "This was caught in the winch."

Detective Hughley and Mr. Potter joined me. The detective took the glove from me.

"This yours?" he asked Mr. Potter.

"No, sir. That looks like a gentleman's glove. Not like the work gloves I use. My gloves are thicker made, and tan colored."

The detective shoved the glove into his coat pocket.

"What are you doing?" I asked.

"I'm taking it to the station. It's evidence." He let out a long breath. "Well, it looks like there is nothing else up here to see. Shall we?" he nodded toward the ladder. He got onto it first and stepped down a few rungs and then looked up at me. "Do be careful, Mrs. Pryce."

The descent was far more terrifying than the ascent, but in a few moments I was down.

"Well?" William said, directing his question to the detective.

"Mrs. Pryce, found a glove in one of the winches," Detective Hughley said.

"That's odd. Could it belong to whomever did this?" William asked.

"Quite possibly."

"What about my ring?" I asked.

"I'll check in with some of the pawnbrokers in the area. See if any of them have seen a ring matching the description." He turned to me. "Do you know it's value?"

I shook my head. "It doesn't matter to me. It has sentimental value."

"Very well." He said with some finality. "I will need to interview all of your cast members and the workers in the theater. It might take some time, but we will get to the bottom of this, Mrs. Pryce."

"I think we should cancel the show," I said with some gravity.

"That would not be wise." The detective shook his head. "You must keep the status quo. It will be easier to find the culprit. The more they think they have things under control, the more opportunity there is for them to make a mistake."

"But what about Arabella's safety?" Cordelia asked.

"I'll make sure nothing happens to her." The detective gave me a warm smile.

CHAPTER 9

The following morning I awoke with dread. I was going to have to give my first performance without the ring in eighteen years. And, based upon rehearsal yesterday, to say that my confidence was crushed would be an understatement.

Adding to that the fact someone wanted me, or William, or both of us, dead, and had hurt Mrs. Greer in the process, did nothing to bring my usual drive to get up and greet the day.

Who would want to kill us? And for what reason? Taking the ring was one thing. It could have been taken for a number of reasons; need, greed, or a punishment of sorts.

My thoughts fell on the latter. If someone wanted to punish me, then my gut feeling that the theft had been deeply personal was correct. There were three people I could think of who might want to punish me. There was Mrs. Greer, of course. She might have taken the ring, but as far as murder was concerned, she had been on the stage with me and William when the rigging fell.

The two others who might have wanted to see me suffer were Maurice and my mother.

Maurice was charming, quick with a laugh, and somewhat bumbling, either due to drink or his laissez-faire attitude. He was also highly sensitive, which contributed to his brilliance as an actor, and could be given to brooding on occasion. I had no doubt that he was thoroughly wounded at the news that William had delivered to him—that he would not be going on tour with us. I could definitely see that he might have taken the ring as a punishment of sorts. But Jacob had said he'd been with Maurice most of the night. Perhaps Maurice had slipped away from the party before he'd gotten so drunk?

And, he had been in the wings shortly after the accident. If he had been up in the rafters, had we been so distracted by the fallen rigging on top of Mrs. Greer that we didn't see him, or hear him descend? But, if he did it, why would he show himself when I called out thinking it was Mr. Potter? I would think that if he did do it, he would have fled. He had not been at the theater since his debauched departure after the party, so had he gone undetected, we would not be the wiser. Then again, showing himself could throw off suspicion.

My mother, on the other hand, might want to see William dead, but she would never harm me physically because I was her only means of income. I was a valuable asset. But he, on the other hand, had taken away her power, and in essence, taken away me. A chill coursed down my spine. I had pushed William out of the way. He had been standing right where the rigging fell.

And the ring? Her stealing it would have definitely restored some of her control over me. If she did steal it, I could see hard line negotiations in my future. And with William gone . . .

Curiosity drove me out of bed. I donned my dressing gown and slippers and made my way to her room that was down at the end of the exceedingly long hallway. Mother had always been an early riser, and liked to take her breakfast downstairs in the sunroom.

Downstairs, the mansion was coming to life with the sounds of the staff already setting to work.

I slipped inside Mother's bedroom. The bed had not yet been made, but embers glowed in the fireplace. Mother liked her fire lit at an impossibly early hour.

I decided to check her jewelry box first. It was neatly arrayed with her vast collection of baubles, but there was no sign of the ring. I searched her wardrobe, her vanity, and even under the mattress to no avail. I then went to the writing desk that was positioned under a window overlooking Central Park. The contents of the drawers were tidily arranged. Papers, writing utensils, one of my scripts, and various odds and ends—including her diary. I lifted it out of the drawer, my stomach swirling with a mixture of curiosity and guilt. I knew it would be a betrayal to open it and read its contents, but there was the corner of a piece of paper sticking out from the bottom of it.

Carefully, I pulled it from the diary without opening the pages. It looked to be a receipt from a Jewelry shop. On closer inspection, it was not a receipt at all, but an appraisal. Dated June 16. Two weeks ago. For a Forget-Me-Not diamond ring. It's value was fifty-two dollars and forty-seven cents. I was a bit surprised that it was not worth more, but diamonds were not nearly as valuable as rubies or emeralds.

Why had she had it appraised? Perhaps in order to secure a little nest-egg for the future? I had earlier considered that Mother might have taken the ring, but this find made it all too real. It sickened me.

I fled the room only to find Cordelia knocking on my bedroom door. Waving the piece of paper I rushed over to her.

"I think I know who stole the ring," I said, tears stinging the back of my eyes.

I showed her the paper.

"Oh, my." She pressed her fingers to her lips.

"I'm going to ask her about this," I stated, my tearful emotion giving way to anger. "How dare she?"

"I'm afraid she isn't here," Cordelia said. "I saw her leaving just a few minutes ago."

"Did she say where she was going?"

Cordelia shook her head. "No, but Arabella, the detective is waiting for you downstairs."

"What? Here?" I asked, a bit alarmed that he would come to my residence. How had he known where I lived? I supposed the police had their ways.

"He wants to escort you to the theater in his carriage."

"Ugh! Really? Why could he not just meet me at the theater?"

She lifted a shoulder. "He's just doing his duty, Arabella. He's concerned for your safety."

"Oh, very well!" I said, feeling a bit flustered. "But you are coming with me. And Bijou, of course. He makes me uncomfortable."

"Of course, dear. Let's get you dressed."

Cordelia, with Bijou on her lap, and I sat opposite Detective Hughley in his carriage. His face was void of his usual besotted smile, and it its place, a look of seriousness, which eased my previous discomfort at the prospect of riding with him to the theater.

"This really wasn't necessary, detective," I said.

"It's no bother, Mrs. Pryce. Especially when the world is at risk of losing such a wonderful talent," he said gravely.

"But, what if the attempt was made on my husband and not me?" I added. "Are you providing him with protection?"

His countenance darkened further. "I have assigned an officer to watch out for him. He will be of no bother to your husband, of course."

"I see," I said. William would not at all like to have a police officer tagging along behind him all day, but needs must, I suppose.

"Mrs. Pryce, do you have any idea at all who might want to harm you?—Or your husband? Have you had any disagreements with anyone of late?"

I explained to him the situation with Maurice. "But, I can't imagine him wanting to kill us." I added. "Yet, he was at the theater. In the wings shortly after the rigging fell. I'm not sure why he was there. He and Theodore Brinks, his understudy, took Mrs. Greer to the hospital."

"And how is she faring?" he asked.

"I have not heard. I intend to check on her today. Wait a minute," I said, remembering what Miss Crookshank had said, but how could I relay this to the detective without mentioning that I often parlayed with a ghost.? "I—I saw Mrs. Greer go up to the catwalk—to dust after the opening night performance, which was an odd time for her to be up there."

"She didn't like Arabella at all." Cordelia piped in.

"You're not saying that she could have cut the ropes?" Detective Hughley rubbed his chin. "But, she was on the stage. Unless . . ."

"What?"

"She had an accomplice. Perhaps she went on stage to ensure you, or your husband, were in the correct position to suffer the rigging."

"Oh, dear" I said. "Her husband. I fired her husband recently."

Cordelia's face paled. "Well—yes, but they wouldn't want to kill you for that? Would they?"

"It's definitely a motive," the detective said. "I will go to the hospital to speak with her. Where might I find her husband?"

"I believe they live at—" Cordelia started. Detective Hughley handed her a small notepad and pencil. She took it and scribbled down the address. "Mrs. Greer might have taken the ring, to sell it," she added.

I shook my head. "If she took it for the money, then why leave my bracelet and gold locket? Whomever took the ring knew what it meant to me." My heart flagged at the thought that it could have been my mother, but I wasn't sure I wanted to voice that to the detective just yet.

"You did ask Mrs. Greer to go to your dressing room to tidy up while we were all enjoying the party in the green room. That's probably where the feather came from," Cordelia added. "Mrs. Greer's feather duster."

"What feather?" the detective asked.

"We found part of an ostrich feather on the floor," she said.

"But, it could have come from any number of people," I added. "Maurice wears two in his Robin Hood hat, although, last I saw one was missing, and Rebecca, the wardrobe mistress, she works with feathers all the time, and then there's . . ."

"Yes?" The detective looked at me expectantly.

My stomach clenched. I did not want to mention my mother and the feather fan, her constant companion, but, how could I stand by if she wanted to be rid of William?

"There is one more person," I said quietly. "My mother. She always carries a fan with her."

His face scrunched up in questionable doubt. "Your mother. You think she means to harm you?"

I handed him the appraisal. "I found this earlier this morning in her room." I then explained mine and William's plan to replace her as my manager. "I hadn't told her about this until recently, but she sensed what was coming. I will always take care of her of course, but I haven't had a chance to talk in depth with her about it. My mother is a very hard woman, detective."

Suddenly wracked with guilt for basically confiding in him that she was a potential thief and could possibly have planned murder, I wanted to take it all back.

"I know she wouldn't want to harm me. She does love me—in her way, and I don't think she would want to harm William, but she might have taken the ring."

Detective Hughley nodded. "All right. I have some officers checking the pawn brokers, to see if the ring has turned up. When we arrive at the theater, I will interview your staff."

"We do have a performance tonight, detective. They might be busy. And the cast will not arrive until early this afternoon. I'm sure they are resting this morning."

"Don't you worry," he said, his face finally breaking into the boyish grin I had seen before. "We will be sensitive to everyone's duties."

"What if the person who cut the ropes of the rigging is at the performance tonight? What if they attempt to harm Arabella?" Cordelia asked.

"I will be there, and a few of my officers as well. We will see that nothing goes amiss." His gaze traveled back to meet mine. "I will let nothing diminish your brilliance."

CHAPTER 10

Once we arrived at the theater, Detective Hughley escorted Cordelia and I to my dressing room. He did a quick search of the place and then took leave of us, for which I was relieved.

"I know he is trying to protect me, but I feel as if he has secured a ball and chain around my ankle," I complained. "You know how I need complete solitude to prepare for a performance—and with him and his officers lurking about, how am I to do that?"

The low level of anxiety I had experienced since the loss of the ring was rising to something a bit less manageable. How was I to perform without it?

"Perhaps we should cancel," I said.

"Cancel? Oh, no, you can't do that," Cordelia said. "The detective said—"

"What if we said I was ill, and could not go on?" I reasoned.

"Come now," she soothed. "You will shine like the sun on stage, like you always do, Arabella. You mustn't let this deter you. And, it would not be prudent to cancel for the reason the detective gave, and because of the fact that the show is sold out again—and we've only just opened."

I heaved a sigh in an attempt to calm the swarm of butterflies that swirled around in my belly.

"I will fetch you some Chamomile tea, dear. That always calms your nerves."

I huffed. "Well, you'd better make a lot of it. I'll need several pots!"

With an endearing chuckle, she left the room.

"Good morning," she said to someone else.

I turned around to see Maurice standing in the doorway. Remembering he had been lurking in the wings when the rigging fell, I was a little disconcerted to be with him alone.

"Maurice, what can I do for you?" I asked, in a business-like tone.

"I've—well, I'd like a word, Arabella." He clutched the Robin Hood hat in his hands. "May I?"

"Of course." I rose and met him at the doorway.

"I wanted to—well, I wanted to apologize for—for not being as professional as I should. I'm sadly disappointed that you will not renew my contract to go on tour with you, but, I can't say as I blame you or your husband."

This was interesting. Maurice, though charming, was exceedingly arrogant and had never apologized for anything. I wondered if he was just trying to get back into my good graces.

"We must be able to rely on all cast members—" I said.

He held up a hand. "I know. And, I've been unreliable at times. I like working with you, Arabella, and your company of players. I'd like a second chance."

I considered his words for a moment. He seemed sincere.

"Have you heard about my ring?" I inquired.

He nodded. "Yes, Jacob told me. Bit of bad luck, eh?"

"Yes. The theft feels quite personal. Whomever took it knew *exactly* what it meant to me." I eyed the hat between his hands. He followed my gaze, and then looked up at me again.

"You don't think—?" His face took on a wounded expression. He shook his head. "I'm a lot of things, Arabella, but I'm not a thief. I would never do that to you—knowing what that ring means to you."

I had a feeling I could believe him, but wasn't sure I could trust that feeling quite yet.

"The detective just left here, has he spoken to you? About what happened with Mrs. Greer?"

He shook his head. "No."

That's odd, I thought. It seemed based on when the detective left and Maurice arrived, they might have run into each other. But, perhaps not.

"What were you doing in the theater, right before the rigging fell?" I ventured.

"I—I was coming to see you. To speak with you, but when I got here, well, everyone was worried about what had happened. I didn't get the chance."

"So you weren't here before it fell?"

"No. I came in right behind Potter. You can ask him."

So, like Mr. Potter, he couldn't have had time to go up and cut the ropes.

"Thank you, Maurice. For the apology. We can talk more about this later."

He gave me that award-winning smile of his. "You're welcome. I'll see you on stage."

I watched him leave and slip into his dressing room. His heartfelt apology went a long way with me. If he truly did like working with me, and the others, then why would he do something as spiteful as taking the ring, and as vengeful as wanting to kill either me or William? He obviously wanted to get back into my good books, probably with the hope of working with me again. I would have to think about this.

But for now, all I could think of was my impeding performance.

After several minutes, Cordelia returned with a tray laden with a pot of tea, a creamer of milk, a teacup and saucer, and a biscuit. I turned to her with what must have been a stricken expression on my face.

"You all right, Arabella?"

"No," I gave a half-hearted chuckle. "Far from it. And, I have a headache. The tea will fix me up," I resolved. "I must rehearse . . ."

"I'll leave you to it," she said with a smile and left the room again.

I poured myself a cup of tea, and sat on the settee sipping the lukewarm liquid. The theater was often so drafty, it was hard to keep anything warm. The taste of the chamomile soured in my mouth.

Unable to relax, I rose from my perch and paced the floor, going over my lines in my head—but, I kept forgetting them, and each time I forgot a word, or a phrase, my anxiety rose. Moisture bloomed under my arms and my hands tingled with heat. Feeling a bit unsteady, I pressed a palm to my forehead.

"I used to fall apart before a performance, too," a soft voice echoed in the room. I stopped pacing to see Leticia Crookshank perched where I had just been on the settee.

I shook my head. "But, you don't understand—I *never* fall apart before a performance. I am always so ready, as if I am armed for battle and anxious to get into the fray. This is not me."

"My dear, someone tried to harm you, or your husband, on the very stage where you are to perform. It's quite understandable that you are upset."

"I am upset about that, of course, but I am also upset about the fact that I have lost myself to that stupid ring!"

Her ghostly face took on an expression I had not seen in her before—one of impatience. "Nonsense," she said. "You must never think that. You are not lost to anything or anyone, Arabella. Now, stop this fretting and let's go over your lines."

I raised my hands in the air and then let them drop to my sides. "But, I can't remember them."

"Look at your script," she said.

"No. No! I refuse. I know these lines like I know my own face."

"Then let's go over them. I'll pay Robin Hood." She smiled.

"But, do you know his lines?"

She let go a laugh. "What do you think I do all day? Nap? Of course I know the lines. I know this play backwards and forwards. Now—I believe you have the opening line?" She regarded me with raised, transparent brows.

We spent the next several hours rehearsing. Occasionally she would give me some instruction, or piece of advice, that miraculously made me feel completely connected with the story, and to the character. For that two hours, I was living in Nottinghamshire at its beloved Sherwood Forrest. It was magical.

When I finished my last line for the second time, I let out a satisfied breath.

"Feeling better?" she asked.

"I don't know how to thank you."

"I'll tell you how. Break a leg tonight." She drifted up from the sofa toward the ceiling and then, in a blink, she was gone.

Before I could even turn around, Detective Hughley came into the room.

"Excuse me!" I snapped, affronted that the man didn't even bother to knock. What if I had been in a state of undress?

"Forgive me, Mrs. Pryce. I heard your voice raised and was afraid you were in danger."

"Oh," I said, panic rising in my chest. "I—I was rehearsing."

He cocked his head. "It sounded as if you were conversing with someone."

"No. No, I was playing opposite myself. I often do that to better immerse myself in the story."

"I see," he looked at me rather skeptically. "Pardon the intrusion, but I have some news."

"Did you speak with Mrs. Greer?"

He shook his head. "I arrived at the hospital at an inopportune time. It seems she also sustained injury to her head. She's been in and out of consciousness."

"Oh, dear," Cordelia said.

"Did you find Mr. Greer?" I asked.

He pressed his lips together. "I did. It seems he has been down at the jail for the past couple of days. For assaulting a patron of a drinking establishment."

"So, he couldn't have cut the rigging?"

"No."

"I see. How was he? Did you tell him the news of his wife?"

"I did. He was distraught, as you can imagine."

"Poor man." I made a mental note to have Cordelia pay him his wife's wages—and to pay for her medical care.

"I have news about your ring." The detective broke my train of thought.

My heart lifted and I moved closer to him. "Really? What is it?"

"One of the pawnbrokers received a ring—a Forget-Me-Not ring fashioned with small diamonds."

"That's it! That's it Detective Hughley. Do you have it?"

He pressed his lips together and shook his head. "I'm afraid not. It was sold shortly after he obtained it."

My spirits flagged. "It's sold? Does he know who purchased it? I'll pay double what they paid for it."

"He said he'd never seen the man before, and he didn't get his name."

I went over to the settee, the euphoric feeling I'd had while rehearsing with Leticia Crookshank gone—like it was in a far-off dream. Tears pricked behind my eyes and stung the back of my nose. My ring was gone. Gone forever. And with it, any connection to my father, whose whereabouts had been long unknown. My heart broke with grief.

Detective Hughley removed his hat, releasing his wild mane of waves. He came to sit next to me. "There's more."

I shook my head, not sure I wanted to hear more.

"The person who sold the ring to the pawn dealer was a woman. A woman matching the description of your mother."

The news hit me like a blow to the stomach.

I sucked in a breath and then bit my lip in order to suppress the tears that threatened to release themselves down my cheeks. I suppose I wasn't surprised, but it still hurt. How could she have done something so awful? So cruel?

Detective Hughley, compassion in his eyes, reached up and was about to touch my face but I pulled back.

"I beg your pardon."

"Forgive me. It just grieves me to see you in such pain, Arabella."

I stood up. "Mrs. Pryce," I reminded him.

He, too, rose from the settee. "Of course, Mrs. Pryce." He said with apology.

He cleared his throat and then continued. "I'm afraid your mother might also be responsible for the fallen rigging."

"What? That can't be true. I can believe that she sold my ring—but, try to kill me?"

"I believe it's your husband she is after. Both you and your husband explained to me that he was replacing her as your manager, and that your mother is very upset about it. That she wants complete control over you and your career."

"Well—yes, but?" Granted, the same idea had crossed my mind before, that Mother wanted to be rid of William, but it was just a passing thought. She, indeed, was a formidable figure and always found a way to get what she wanted, but stoop to murder? It couldn't be true.

"We found evidence," he said quietly.

"What evidence?" I spat—still unwilling to believe this impossible scenario.

"We found a man's black glove in her possession. In her handbag."

My heart fell to the pit of my stomach.

And then I remembered. In her intense desire to control

everything about this particular show, she had taken several trips up to the catwalk to inspect the positioning of the backdrops. She was familiar with the equipment up there.

My mouth dropped open and I gasped for breath, the stays of my corset suddenly growing too tight, as if they would strangle me. The room spun and I faltered back toward the settee.

Then, the last thing I remember was falling into the arms of Detective Hughley.

CHAPTER 11

"Darling. My dear girl." The sound of my father's voice roused me. "The truth is closer than you think."

"Arabella. Arabella." I opened my eyes to find that I was prostrate on the settee, my head resting in Cordelia's lap. Her hands were cupped around my face. Bijou had risen up on her hind feet and rested her paws on my shoulder. She emitted a small, but very concerned whine.

"What happened?" I said, attempting to rise, but Cordelia pressed down on my shoulders.

"Lie still a moment. Detective Hughley has gone to fetch you a glass of water. You fainted."

"Fainted?" I found the strength to sit up. "I've never fainted in my life."

"The detective said you were overcome by emotion . . ."

And, then I remembered. The detective had said he'd found evidence that my mother had been the one responsible for cutting the rigging, that she had tried to kill my husband.

"Yes, I—"

"What is all of this?" My mother marched into the room with the detective and Officer Trent on her heels. "Arabella, darling, are you all right?" She rushed over to me and sat down, sandwiching me between her and Cordelia. "Are you ill?"

I wriggled out from between the two of them and stood up. Still a little unsteady, I swayed and Detective Hughley took hold of my elbow. I pulled away from him.

"Only ill at ease." I said flatly, my ire rising at the look of mock concern and confusion on my mother's face.

The detective handed me a glass of water, but I refused it.

"Why, Mother?"

"Why what, darling? Come sit. You do not look well. You have your performance tonight and—"

"You took my ring. You sold it. You knew what that ring meant to me. You're jealous. Jealous and possessive!" I couldn't bear to bring up the subject of her potentially trying to kill my husband—I couldn't stomach the idea, much less speak of it.

Her countenance darkened to the color of a dirty wash towel. "How dare you accuse me! You impertinent girl." She stood up and lunged toward me, but the detective stepped in front of her.

"I'm afraid we have found evidence linking you to the attempted murder, madam." The detective said what I could not.

Her eyes grew wide. "What evidence?"

The detective held his hand out to Officer Trent who procured from a manila envelope my mother's hand bag.

She gasped. "Where did you—?"

"I found it at your place of residence."

"You searched our home?" she said with indignation. "What right have you—"

"Probable cause, Mrs. Janes. The maid let me in."

Officer Trent gave over the handbag to the detective who drew from it a man's black leather glove.

"You sent William the note asking him to come to the theater." I realized out loud.

My mother clutched at her throat, her face having gone a sickly shade of gray. "What note? And, I've never seen that glove before—I—"

And, we also know that you sold the ring," the detective said, looming closer to her, towering above her.

She sucked in a breath. "I beg your pardon! Stand aside, sir."

The detective didn't move, but I wormed my way between them. "I found an appraisal for the ring in your desk. You wanted to see it's worth, so that you could sell it when William finally fired you."

"This is preposterous!" she raged. "Yes, I got an appraisal for the ring. I—I wanted to prove that your father's gift was a fake. Just like his affections for you—and for me, as he has proven."

"But, it wasn't fake, was it, Mother? Those diamonds may not be worth as much as rubies or emeralds, but the ring is genuine. Just like my father's love for me."

Her jaw tightened and her eyes flared. "If he loves you so much, then where is he? Where has he been for most of your life? What has he done for you?"

I raised my chin. "He is with me always with that ring. It gave me strength, purpose. And you took that away from me."

"I did not take that ring! And, what have I done for you? Everything! I've done everything for you. I've made you a star."

"By working me to death! You took my childhood from me. It was your glory you were after, not mine."

"I kept you alive!" Her eyes were on fire, and her mouth screwed up into a vengeful sneer. "And protected you from a fate even worse than death. . ."

I knew of what she spoke. Being exposed as someone who thought they could communicate with the dead. Or worse yet, being exposed as someone who actually could. Someone who practiced the art of the occult. Someone who needed to be shut away in an asylum.

As far as she knew, I had only seen Oliver Shrewsbury's ghost —and now, Leticia Crookshank had broken through the wall I had worked so hard to build up. Worry stabbed at my gut that my mother might reveal my sensitivities to the press out of revenge for turning against her. But, hadn't she turned her back on me? The injustice of it all settled on me like a pall.

The detective gently nudged me aside. "Mrs. Millicent Janes, I am arresting you for the attempted murder of William Pryce."

She opened her eyes wide, the rage in them replaced with disbelief. "You cannot do this. Arabella, don't let him do this."

Completely shattered, I found I couldn't speak. I stood my ground and remained silent as he led her away, her protests echoing down the hallway and fading into the bowels of the building. Unable to stop the torrent of emotions—anger, fear, betrayal and sorrow pressing down on me, I crumpled to the floor. In a flash, Cordelia was at my side.

"Oh, my dear, I am so sorry." She smoothed her hand over my hair and I took comfort in her touch, as I always did. What would I do without Cordelia, who was always steadfast, caring, and loyal?

I got myself to my feet and straightened my skirt. Bijou promptly danced on her hind legs, wanting me to pick her up. I complied and nestled my face into her soft fur.

"I need to prepare for tonight." I said quietly, not wanting to think about my mother and her treachery. I couldn't. Not when I had a performance in a matter of hours.

"Arabella, this is too much. Perhaps you should cancel after all." Cordelia reasoned.

"It's too late for that now. The house will be full in just two hours. The show must go on."

<hr />

And, as I had feared, my performance that night was a catastrophe—a reenactment of the previous day's rehearsal. Worse yet, Atticus Brooks, a theater critic well known for his harsh reviews, had been there.

A glance at the newspaper the following morning confirmed

my belief that I was nothing without the ring. The review was scathing.

Completely beside myself, and overrun with a tumult of painful emotions at my mother's betrayal, and worse yet, her prediction of my failure, I fled the mansion to be alone with my anxious thoughts, and to take succor in the only place I felt I was truly myself. The theater.

Standing on the stage, looking out into the empty house, I wanted to scream, to have a temper tantrum, to cry to the Heavens, but the words and the tears wouldn't come. There was nothing left in me. In that performance I had put everything out onto the stage, had given of myself so completely, and yet, that damnable Atticus Brooks had been correct.

My performance had been "Awful. Lackluster. Amateurish." And, as much as I wanted to lash out, to defend myself, to say it wasn't so and that Mr. Brooks was wrong, deep in my heart I knew he wrote the truth.

My fears were coming to pass.

"I heard some of the crew talking about the review this morning.' A gentle voice hovered behind me from above. "It wasn't a fair assessment."

I looked up into the rafters to see Miss Crookshank sitting there, her hoop skirt and petticoats peeking out from under her skirt.

I shook my head in disagreement. "No. He's right. I was terrible."

"We have all experienced a bad night on stage, my dear." She floated downward from above, like a large umbrella alighting to the ground, blanketing me in a cool mist. I shuddered.

She stood next to me with her hands clasped at her waist.

"It's the ring. Without it, I have lost my skills. My talent."

"That simply isn't true," she said. "Your talent and learning lives within you, not in the ring."

I looked over at her indignantly. "If that is so, then why did I give such an abysmal performance?"

"The ring may not possess your talent, but it does possess your confidence. You have given it that power, and the power must be taken back."

An ache at my temples pulsed. I closed my eyes and rubbed them with my fingers. The coolness emanating off my ghostly companion soothed my heated discomfort.

I opened my eyes and lowered my hands. I wandered over to the sofa and sank down onto the lumpy cushions. Miss Crookshank floated after me.

"But, how? I don't know how?" I said. "How will I recover from this? How can I go back on stage tonight? What if no one comes after reading the review? I will never live down the shame. It's ruined. It's all ruined!"

Hovering over me, she let out a small chuckle. "The public will want to see what all the fuss is about. A bad review can sometimes be a blessing, my dear."

I shook my head. "And it won't be long before news of my mother being arrested for attempted murder gets out. I'll never live down the shame of it all. If only I could find the ring. At least I might be able to salvage my career."

"Oh, my goodness!" she said with a chuckle. "You don't think that all of your hard work is for nothing do you? *You* have made your own success, my dear. You have a light within you that shines out onto the world. It's you, Arabella. Not the ring. Not your mother."

I gave her a half-hearted smile. "I appreciate the sympathy, Miss Crookshank. And, I thank you for your guidance—"

"It will always be available to you," she cut in.

"And, for that I am grateful. But, I must find that ring. I'm cancelling the show until I have it back on my finger."

"Don't you think that's running away? Admitting defeat? You mustn't Arabella."

I let go a sigh. She was right, of course. Absolutely right. I had to try. I had to overcome this fear, this attachment to the ring. What if I never found it? Did that mean that I would give up my art? Give up everything I knew?

I took in a deep breath and closed my eyes once again. When I opened them, she was gone.

William strode toward me.

"Hello, darling," he said with a tone of sympathy in his voice. From my vantage point, from where I was sitting, he was tall, imposing, and magnificent. And to think, I had almost lost him. It made me shudder.

"You've seen the review?" I asked.

He nodded. "Yes. That man is a fool. I'm afraid the review might have been on my account."

I said up straight. "Yours? What do you mean?"

"He was at the club—as a guest of course. The man has no standing in society that would afford him to be a member. Anyway, he's friendly with one of my colleagues, and that colleague invited him to join our card game at the club. The man was cheating and I called him out on it."

"Oh, dear," I said.

"Had him thrown out, actually."

My shoulders sagged. "Why did you do that?"

Of course the man was angry. I'd like to think that was the real reason, but the reality that I simply had not performed up to par still lurked in my heart.

"I couldn't allow a card cheat to remain at our table," William said. "He needed to be shown the door. At any rate, I am sorry darling. I will see that he is fired."

I gasped. "What? Fired? No! That would make things worse. Besides, how would you do that?"

He shrugged. "I am on friendly terms with the owner and editor of *The Stage Guild*. He owes me a favor. I can see to it that Brooks is never published again in New York."

I sighed. This would not do. It would shine a bad light upon me. Worse than the one that was already highlighting my dreadful performance. I shook my head. "No, dear. Leave the man alone. Please inform Mr. Blackthorn that I am cancelling the show until I find the ring. He can make some excuse for the patrons—that I'm ill or something."

Which in truth, I was. Ill at the fact that I had never delivered such a ghastly performance before, and ill at the notion that my mother, in her jealousy, had meant to do William, and me, harm—both emotionally and physically. The fear that she might yet reveal my secret to the world threatened to crush my very soul—it was almost too much to think about.

"Cancelling? Don't you think that is a bit extreme, my dear? I don't think it is a wise business decision."

"Please William. I cannot perform tonight. My heart isn't in it, and I'm afraid I might be worse than last night, and *that* would not be good for business."

He sighed. "You know your own mind, dear. I won't interfere with your decision—even if I do not agree with it. I suppose it is for the best as I am leaving for La Plata Springs tomorrow. I say —since you are thinking of cancelling the show, why don't you come with me? It would do you well to get away from all of this mess."

I gave him a dubious look. "I—I don't think so, dear."

"Come on! The Southwestern region of the country is beautiful, darling. Rugged, purple mountain peaks, azure skies, fire-y sunsets. It's absolutely magical. A cure for any ill—"

I held up a hand, unable to bear the thought. "No, William. I wish to stay here and find my ring."

He opened his mouth to protest, but I shook my head. "Please."

He sighed. "Very well."

"Thank you."

"Then, will you at least come home and rest. You can look for your ring tomorrow."

"No. I will summon Detective Hughley. I want to ask him which pawnbroker purchased the ring from Mother."

Feeling utterly wretched, I parted ways with him and went to my dressing room to dash off a note to the eager detective.

CHAPTER 12

I sat at my vanity with my head in my hands. It throbbed with a dull ache, and my stomach felt as if a large stone had taken up residence in it, filling it with its terrible weight.

I thought about my mother. Guilt and sorrow stabbed at my heart. The stricken look on her face when she had vehemently denied both allegations was heartbreaking. I was feeling so many things I wanted to escape my own skin and run off to some foreign place where none of this could find me. Somewhere other than the godforsaken wilds of Colorado!

I still could not quite believe that my mother, the one who had given me life, the one who had been so determined to see me succeed—for whatever reason (I too had greatly benefitted from her tenacity and ambitions) would want to kill my husband to secure her place in my career.

But both Detective Hughley and I had found solid evidence that she had taken the ring, and had tried to kill William.

Yet something just didn't feel right. I gathered it wasn't supposed to *feel right* when one's mother might have done such horrible things. Or even that one's mother was in jail. No matter how close or estranged one was with their parent, there was always that singular thread of connection that pulled at one's heartstrings for them, as I knew so well with my father.

An ache for him bloomed in my chest. If he were here, he would make everything all right. He would give me the comfort and strength I needed. He believed in me, more than I believed in myself.

If only I could find the ring, it would bring him closer. It would give me the strength to overcome my lack of confidence. And, perhaps, help me to overcome the hold my mother had over me.

Sitting at my vanity, I hastily scrawled a message to Detective Hughley and then gave it to one of the crew to deliver to the station.

When I returned to my dressing room, I was greeted by Miss Crookshank, who was standing near my vanity, hands poised at her waist, looking as if she was preparing to belt out a soliloquy.

"Hello," I said, less than enthusiastically.

"You look like Atlas holding up the weight of the world." The sympathy in her smile made me want to crawl inside myself. I went to the vanity and sat down. "I feel wretched."

"Do you really believe that your mother would want to hurt you so?"

"I don't want to believe it, but how can I refute the evidence? She was so angry at William, and at me. In hindsight, I see that replacing her with William and Blackthorn was stripping her of the one thing she has striven to do my entire life. I was denying her what she feels is her purpose. But, it had to be done. I was suffocating. It was my only way out from under that burden."

"Don't be too hard on yourself, dear. Everyone must separate from their parents, painful as it can be sometimes."

"It's not that I didn't want her in my life. I do. I love her. I just wanted her to be my mother, not my manager. But, apparently, she did not know how to do that." The back of my eyes stung with the threat of tears. I didn't want to cry. I would not cry. For if I let one tear escape, it would open the floodgates and I would drown in my sorrow.

I leaned my elbows on the vanity and place my aching head between my fingers and pressed them hard into my temples, trying to relieve the pressure.

"That is supposed to have medicinal qualities," Miss Crookshank said. "Did you purchase it?"

I looked over at her and she was pointing to the bottle of Florida Water. I reached out and opened it, and an invisible cloud of fragrance surrounded me. It was a pleasant aroma, with notes of citrus and herbs, along with spice and floral undertones —and it was so familiar.

"No. It was one of the gifts left after the opening night performance."

The flash of a memory struck me.

I offered my hand. He took it and planted a faint kiss upon my knuckles. I noticed that he kept his other hand tucked in the pocket of his coat. The scent of the roses mingled with another pleasing aroma that seemed to emanate from him. It was a mixture of fruit and dry spice, like cloves —or perhaps cinnamon. He pulled his face away, but did not let go of my hand.

"What a lovely ring," he said, admiring it. "Is this the one you always wear on stage?"

"Detective Hughley," I said out loud.

"What about him?" Miss Crookshank asked.

"Cordelia had mentioned a pleasant fragrance when we'd gone in the dressing room to find the ring gone. I was so upset I didn't notice, but—"

Rebecca had said he was waiting outside the door of my dressing room to see me. He must have gone in when she went to fetch me.

"He'd professed his 'passionate admiration' for me," I continued. "He wanted me to disregard my marriage. When I refused —" I sucked in a breath.

I glanced over at the funeral hat, and sitting next to it was the clipped Ostrich feather Cordelia had found on the floor. The one that resembled the feathers in Mother's fan, and Mrs. Greer's duster, and Maurice's Robin Hood hat.

An image of Detective Hughley that night resurfaced in my mind. He'd worn that strange-looking fluffy boutonniere on his lapel. I realized it now. It had been fashioned from ostrich feathers.

"The funeral hat and note of condolences was for William. It was him," I said under my breath. "It was him all along."

Miss Crookshank vanished and I sensed a presence behind me.

"Who?" A male voice behind me startled me. I turned to see Detective Hughley standing in my doorway.

CHAPTER 13

My throat went dry and fear pricked at the back of my neck.

"It was you."

He stepped into the room and closed the door behind him. He planted himself in front of it, his imposing figure blocking it from view. His left hand was placed in his coat pocket, as was his custom, and it dawned on me. The glove with the stuffed pinky finger.

"The glove is yours."

He remained fixed at the door, his face placid, blank, devoid of anything.

"You knew about my troubles with my mother. You knew the depth of her anger. She made the perfect villain."

"I knew you wanted your freedom," he finally said. "I was trying to free you from her."

"And from my husband?" I glanced over at the funeral hat.

He chuckled. "Pretty, isn't it? I thought you would look most fetching in it for your husband's funeral. My plan didn't quite work out. But, don't worry. I'll make sure to get rid of him. He's leaving for Colorado, I believe? What a coincidence. I have a friend taking the same train tomorrow—"

My heart plummeted to the pit of my stomach. "No!" I said. "Leave William alone!"

He tilted his head. "That could be arranged."

"What do you mean?"

"Leave him, Arabella. Be with me. And he will be safe and your mother won't bother you anymore.

"I'm not going anywhere with you!" I ground out.

"But, why? Don't you see how much I love you?" He moved toward me and I backed away.

"You tried to kill my husband! And you injured an innocent woman!" I shouted.

He sighed. "Yes. It is a pity. If only she hadn't stepped in the way of dear William—"

"You are a beast!" I said.

His lower lip protruded in a pout. "You haven't really given me a chance, Arabella."

I scanned the room, looking for some kind of weapon. Rebecca often left a pair of scissors here, but I had never paid attention to where she might keep them.

"He's not right for you, Arabella. I know you do not love him—that your marriage is void of passion."

"You know *nothing* of my marriage." I spat, his words making me uncomfortable, for he was not off the mark about the lack of passion in my marriage. It chilled me to the core that he could somehow see right through me.

"Come away with me," he said, moving closer.

I stood up, facing him, the back of my legs pressed against the vanity.

"I can make you happy. I can give you passion," he said. "You are all I think about. I adore you, don't you see?"

"You tried to kill my husband!" I repeated. "You nearly killed me in the process. That's not love. That's delusion."

"Arabella—" He moved closer and I scooted away from the vanity and stood behind the settee.

"Don't come near me." How I wish I knew where Rebecca

kept the scissors! My gaze fell on the raised dais in front of the mirror, where she often fitted me into my costumes. The glint of something metal peeked out from under the mirror.

"You set up my mother," I said, wanting to keep the conversation going. I slowly inched my way toward the mirror. "I stupidly told you she'd had the ring appraised. There was no visit from your officers to the pawnbroker, was there? But, you didn't lie about searching the mansion. You went there to get one of her handbags."

He moved closer to me, the settee sandwiched between us. I could smell the fragrance of Florida Water on him. He smiled and removed his hat with his free hand and tossed it onto the settee cushions. From the hand in his pocket, he produced the ring. I sucked in a breath. As I had suspected, his pinky finger was merely a stub.

"Why did you take it?" I said.

"Because it has your heart. I wanted it near me."

I gritted my teeth together, disgusted at his obsession. "You're sick."

His smile faded and he lunged for me. I thrust the settee forward, knocking him off balance. I lunged for the scissors, but before I could get to them, he reached under his coat and pulled a pistol from his side holster.

"I thought you would be reasonable, Arabella. I thought you would see how much I love you, and how our life together could be so beautiful."

From behind him, the door opened. It was Cordelia.

In a flash, the detective surged forward, grabbed me and pressed the gun to my temple. Unable to speak, or even to breathe, I froze in his grasp. The sound of my pulse roared in my ears and pinpricks of fear scuttled over my skin.

Cordelia's mouth gaped open and her skin grew sallow. Officer Trent came up behind her.

"What's—?" He started, wide-eyed.

Still holding me hard to his chest, the detective removed the gun from my temple and pointed it at them. "Don't say a word. Step inside and close the door."

They did what he said.

"What is the meaning of this, detective?" Officer Trent asked.

"Shut up," the detective waved the gun toward the center of the room. "Move away from the door."

They did as he said. Cordelia and I made eye contact and I directed my gaze toward the scissors on the dais. Her eyes followed.

"Say one word, and I'll kill her." Detective Hughley placed the tip of the gun barrel back to my head making my heart stop. He pulled me toward the door.

"He's confessed to everything!" I said.

"Be quiet, my darling." The detective pressed the gun harder into my temple.

"This is madness, detective. You don't really think you can get away with this," Officer Trent said.

"If you're dead, I can," he pointed the gun at the officer again. "Remove your weapon and put it on the ground."

Holding his hands in the air, Officer Trent then reached around and release his Billy club from his belt. It fell to the floor."

Suddenly, a cool draft permeated the room sending a chill down my spine and making goose pimples rise on my skin. Miss Crookshank, in all her glory, appeared above the officer and Cordelia's heads. Her eyes glowed with fire and she opened her mouth in a rictus of horror. Her hands rose up like claws.

"What the—" Detective Hughley, mesmerized by the visage, loosened his grip on me. Taking advantage of the situation, I thrust my elbow into his stomach. He clutched over and I was able to grab the gun from his hand. I backed away and stood next to Cordelia and the officer who had picked up his club.

The detective's face had gone ashen, his eyes fixed on Miss Crookshank.

"What's wrong with him?" Cordelia whispered.

Officer Trent took the gun from my hand, and apprehended the detective.

"Sir, you are under arrest for theft, the attempted murder of Arabella Pryce and William Pryce, and the assault of Mrs. Ellen Greer," he said, and escorted him from the room.

CHAPTER 14

Rebecca tugged at the ties at the back of the kirtle, cinching me in tightly. "Goodness, it seems I'm having to lace this more snuggly than usual," she said, a little breathless with the effort.

My hands at my waist, I pressed in on the garment in an effort to help her. "I haven't eaten much in the last couple of days."

"Yes, it's been a trying time for you."

"You as well," I remarked. Rebecca's daughter, Althea, had been in the hospital for a few days. The poor girl's condition had worsened. "Is your daughter home from the hospital?"

"Yes, ma'am. Just yesterday."

I turned around abruptly, inadvertently yanking the ties from her hands. "You should be with her," I said, a little alarmed.

"But, the show, ma'am." She said, turning me back around to start the tying process all over again. "It's all right. She is resting and Priscilla is very attentive. I've told Naomi, my middle daughter, to send for me if I'm needed."

"Your girls are good girls." Sadness crept its way into my heart. Rebecca seemed to have such a nice relationship with her daughters. Their life was not an easy one, much as mine and

Mother's had been when I was young. But our misfortunes had only served to harden us to one another, instead of bringing us closer like Rebecca and her girls.

"And your mother?" Rebecca asked. "Will she be here for the performance?"

"She is being released from police custody as we speak." In all honesty, I would be surprised if she came tonight—or ever again. Shame washed over me at my accusations towards her. I had been so wrapped up in the loss of the ring, that I had lost sight of things. And Detective Hughley had orchestrated his plan so cleverly.

"There." Rebecca straightened the collar of the chemise under the kirtle. "You look a picture."

"Thank you, Rebecca."

"And, so does Maurice. Quite bright eyed, I might add," she said with a smile.

I nodded. "I told him I'd give him another chance—on the condition that he cut back on the drinking, for which he agreed.

He'll be joining us on tour, after all. As Mr. Brink's understudy. It will be a good way for him to prove himself."

"I'm glad to hear it. It would be a shame if you two didn't work together anymore."

"I quite agree," I said.

"I'll leave you, now. Just call for me if you need anything more." Rebecca, and the others knew that before I went on stage, I liked to be alone with a cup of tea. I went to the pot that Cordelia had made for me and poured a cuppa.

The laces had been drawn so tight, it was difficult to sit, but I managed. Holding the teacup to my face, I closed my eyes and let the steam wash over it. It's soothing warmth and calming fragrance began to do its work.

The sound of the door opening disrupted my ritual. I turned to see my mother enter.

I set the teacup down and stood to face her. Her skin was

milk-pale, and her eyes bore a weariness that I had never seen in them before—even during some of our hardest times.

"Mother, I am so terribly sorry for this misunderstanding."

"You clearly don't trust me, Arabella." The hurt in her voice tugged at my heart.

"But, I do—I—you've just been so angry with me and with William, and with our decision that I—And I was so upset about the ring, I—well—I lost all sense. "

"So, it's final. I am to be replaced. Tossed out of your life."

I went to her and took hold of her hands. They were cold, and bony. I gripped them firmly. "You will never be out of my life, Mother. I will always take care of you. But I need this change. I'm thirty years old. I need to grow up. Make my own decisions. Take charge of my own career."

She turned her head away from me, but made no effort to release her hands. "So, what am I to do?" Her gaze returned to mine.

I smiled broadly at her and squeezed her hands. "Enjoy your life. Make friends. Go to the museum. Take long carriage rides in the park. You don't have to work anymore, Mother. Don't you see? With this decision, we are *both* free."

She didn't respond, but returned the squeeze of my hands. A faint upturning of her lips showed her acceptance, albeit reluctantly. She raised her chin and pulled her hands away.

"Very well." Her tone was a little icy, but she was a proud woman. This was not easy for her. "You must prepare."

"Yes," I said, my voice a little shaky. I had the ring back, but still, I was nervous, having done so poorly the night before.

Suddenly she reached out and with the tip of her finger, lifted my chin and settled her gaze on mine. "You are brilliant, Arabella. And, don't you ever forget it. You don't need some trinket to make you so."

I sucked in a breath and blinked back tears, afraid they might ruin my makeup. She gave me a tight smile and left the room.

"She's right you know." Coolness enveloped me and I turned

to see Miss Crookshank lounging on the settee. "Are you quite all right? You seem a little adrift."

I shook my head. "I'm just surprised. My mother is not one to say those kinds of things. As a child, I always strove so hard to make her proud of me. It always felt so out of reach."

I then remembered what my father used to say. *It's never enough. No matter what I do, it's never enough.*

"Some people have a hard time expressing their feelings. It doesn't mean they don't feel them. She *is* proud of you."

I sucked in a breath, afraid the threat of tears might return.

"Will your husband be here tonight?" she asked.

"No. He's gone to Colorado."

"How lovely," she giggled. "I always wanted to go out West. To see that wide open country, those majestic mountains. Have you been?"

I snorted. "No. I don't wish to travel to a place so uncivilized. I like city life."

"But, aren't you curious about the hotel? It would be so exciting to see it, don't you think?"

"No, I don't think. This hotel William has built out there is just one of his passing fancies. I'm sure he will tire of it and then sell it and I will never have to set foot in it."

She shook her head, laughing. "One thing I've learned in life, and in death, is never to say never, my dear."

I snorted again, rolling my eyes. She pointed at the clock hanging on the wall on the opposite side of the room.

"You'd best get out there."

I pinched my cheeks with my thumbs and forefingers to bring up their color. I then went to the drawer where I kept the jewelry box and set it on my vanity. I opened the lid and took out the ring.

I gazed at it for a moment, admiring its beauty and the memories it held. It was heart-shaped, and in the center, the Forget-Me-Not flower. Its five petals were fashioned from diamonds and its leaves, one each on either side of its golden stems had two diamonds encrusted in each one of them.

I clasped it in my palms and held it to my chest. I closed my eyes and thought of my father, wondering where he was, wondering if he was happy. Knowing, that wherever he might be, and whether or not I would ever see him again, he would never forget me, nor I him.

I lowered my hands from my chest, opened my palm, and gazed at the ring one more time before I carefully lowered it back into the jewelry box and closed the lid.

I took in a deep breath, mustering all the courage I could. I turned and faced Miss Crookshank who had floated toward the door.

"Shall we?" She asked.

I gave her a firm nod.

She reached out with her transparent hand, cupping my chin. An icy coolness drifted over my face, soothing the heat of my anxiety. Her transparent features softened and her face glowed with compassion, encouragement and affection.

"Break a leg, darling."

Continue with Arabella's adventures!

Thrown from the theaters of New York into the wilds of Colorado, can one ambitious actress play detective when she's accused of murder? *The Pryce of Conceit* is the suspenseful first book in The Pryce of Murder historical ghost cozy mystery series.

Scan the QR code on the next page to order your copy today!

Have you signed up for my email list? Scan the QR Code below to to check out the Free Books page on my website. You can sign up by selecting a prequel novella to one of my other series.

I love to connect with my readers, and email is the best, most authentic way for us to get to know one another better. You'll also be the first to know about new releases, exciting giveaways, events and other fun stuff!

Did you enjoy *The Pryce of Delusion?* If so, you might want to share the love with other readers. The best way to do that is to leave a review. You don't have to write much, just a few sentences about your reading experience.

You can leave your review and/or star rating on BookBub, Goodreads Amazon and other book retailers.

ABOUT THE AUTHOR

Empowered women in history, horses, unconventional characters, and real-life historical events fill the pages of award-winning author Kari Bovée's articles and historical mystery musings and manuscripts.

She and her husband, Kevin, spend their time between their horse property in the beautiful Land of Enchantment, New Mexico, and their condo on the sunny shores of Kailua-Kona, Hawaii.

Copyright © 2023 by Kari Bovée

Published by Bosque Publishing

ISBN-13: 978-1-947905-22-1 (e-bk)

ISBN-13: 978-1-947905-23-8 (p-bk)

All rights reserved.

No part of this book may be reproduced in any form or by any electronic or mechanical means, including information storage and retrieval systems, without written permission from the author, except for the use of brief quotations in a book review.

This is a work of fiction. Names, characters, places, and incidents either are the product of the author's imagination or are used fictitiously. Any resemblance to actual persons, living or dead, is entirely coincidental.

KariBovee.com

ALSO BY KARI BOVÉE

The Grace Michelle Mysteries

The Annie Oakley Mystery Series

A Ruby Delgado Mystery
A Southwestern Stand Alone
Bones of the Redeemed

Made in United States
Cleveland, OH
02 July 2025